"It's over between us. Can't you accept that?"

At Megan's whispered plea, Devlin's face went frighteningly rigid, his mouth a hard white line. "No." The word had a volcanic force, and she began to shake. "No!" he repeated vehemently, and bent toward her. "I don't let go of anything I still want, Megan, and I don't accept that it's over. It won't be over until I say so."

He straightened, and said in a level tone, "Dinner tonight, Megan, or..."

"Or what?" she said. She tried to sound offhand, indifferent, but her voice wavered. He smiled then, a hard twist of his mouth that was really no smile at all.

Megan knew she'd have to go with him. She had no choice. But she was furious. Devlin's blackmail might get her to dinner...but no further!

CHARLOTTE LAMB began to write "because it was one job I could do without having to leave the children." Now writing is her profession. She has had more than forty Harlequin novels published since 1978. "I love to write," she explains, "and it comes very easily to me." She and her family live in a beautiful old home on the Isle of Man, between England and Ireland. Charlotte spends eight hours a day working at her typewriter—and enjoys every minute of it.

Books by Charlotte Lamb

Don't miss any of our special offers. Write to us at the following address for information on our newest releases.

Harlequin Reader Service
901 Fuhrmann Blvd., P.O. Box 1397, Buffalo, NY 14240
Canadian address: P.O. Box 603,
Fort Erie, Ont. L2A 5X3

CHARLOTTE LAMB

desperation

Harlequin Books

TORONTO • NEW YORK • LONDON
AMSTERDAM • PARIS • SYDNEY • HAMBURG
STOCKHOLM • ATHENS • TOKYO • MILAN

Harlequin Presents first edition September 1989
ISBN 0-373-11202-5

Original hardcover edition published in 1988
by Mills & Boon Limited

CHAPTER ONE

MEGAN CARR slid out of the open french
windows on to the raised stone-paved terrace
and stood there, her pale face, framed in long,
dark hair, lifted to the rising moon. It was a
calm, clear night in late September during one of
those unpredictable spells of warm weather that
can make autumn one of the loveliest of seasons.
Behind Megan buzzed the noise of the party:
loud music, laughter, insistent voices trying to
be heard above the rest. Everyone in there was
having a great time, but she had come out to
escape the gaiety. It grated on her own mood.
Tonight she was melancholy.

'What are you doing out here? You haven't got
a headache, have you?'

The deep voice behind her made her stiffen,
but she did not turn. She didn't need to; she
knew who had followed her out here, and
perhaps she had been hoping that he would,
although torture wouldn't have wrung the
admission out of her.

'No, I'm fine. I just wanted to . . .' Her husky
voice died away as Devlin Hurst came up close
behind her.

'Get away from that racket?' he asked, a smile
in that deep, dark voice of his, and Megan
pretended to laugh.

'Well, it is more peaceful out here!' Although the tranquillity had been blown to smithereens the moment Dev had come out here and sent her temperature climbing, had made her pallor become a burning flush.

'A full moon tonight!' he said, his hands resting lightly on her bare shoulders. Megan shivered at the brush of his skin on her own.

'Cold?' he asked with concern. She hurriedly shook her head, but he turned her to face him, lifted her chin so that her blue eyes had to look up at him. He was a head taller; a man of commanding height who would have been daunting even if he hadn't had such incisive features. Megan had only known him for a couple of months, but she was already in love with him, and the explosive mixture of pain and passion showed in her flushed face.

'What's the matter, Megan?' he asked, and she started to speak half-way through the question, her voice unsteady.

'Nothing! Don't bother about me, go back to the party and your friends.'

'I've talked to them all,' Dev said, grey eyes cool. 'There's nothing more to say to them.'

'You're impatient to be on your way to South America, I suppose,' Megan said, trying to sound light-hearted.

'Yes and no,' he shrugged. 'I am looking forward to reaching the Amazon. This extended trip is the fulfilment of a lifetime's dream. For years I've wanted to explore the river from the source to the river-mouth.' He looked down into her eyes, his mouth crooked. 'But there are some things I'll miss, and I'll be away for a whole year!'

Her lip trembled for a split second and she looked away. 'A year's a long time.' When she thought of the next twelve months, they seemed endless. 'You're going to miss your family,' she said, then over his shoulder she saw the house. Hurst Manor had been in his family for nearly two hundred years, and had all of the solid, comfortable elegance of the eighteenth century.

'I'll miss you!' Dev said, and Megan caught her breath, her face rigid with shock and incredulity.

Dev laughed suddenly at her expression, then stopped short, his hands coming up to frame her face.

'I mean it, you know. I am going to miss you.'

She couldn't speak, only stare, and after a charged silence he bent his head to kiss her. Her eyes closed, her arms went round his neck, a fire between them as their mouths mingled. It wasn't the first time he had kissed her, but this time it was different; this time she was dizzy with pleasure, and Dev's lips were so fierce they almost hurt.

She felt his fingers winding through her long, fine, black hair. From the beginning her hair had seemed to fascinate him; he had stared at it the day she lunched with him that first time, for the TV chat show on which she worked as a researcher. As they left the restaurant Dev had taken a white rose from the vase of flowers on the table and gently pushed it into her hair. 'I love long hair,' he had said as they shared a taxi later. 'It's so sexy; all those amazing swirls and strands floating around your face every time you turn your head.' She had been breathless; no man had ever said such things to her, but then she had never met a man like Devlin Hurst before. Perhaps she had begun to fall in love at that moment.

Dev's mouth reluctantly released hers, and she leaned on him, shuddering with feeling.

'I didn't mean to let go like that,' Dev said thickly. 'I'll be away so long! It wouldn't be fair to ask you . . .' His voice broke off, his white teeth clenching.

'What?' Megan shakily whispered. 'As me what, Dev?'

His eyes moved over her face and her knees turned to water at that look, then Dev shook his head grimly.

'No, I've no right!'

Megan knew she should accept that; of course it was stupid to get seriously involved with a man who was about to go away for a year, especially as they had known each other so short a time anyway, but she knew, too, that she loved him and that time wouldn't change that; neither time nor absence.

'Ask me, Dev,' she said huskily, everything she felt in her blue eyes, and he looked down at her, his face full of conflict. 'Oh, Dev, I love you,' she whispered, and then he began to kiss her again, holding her so tightly she could scarcely breathe.

It seemed a long time later that he asked her. 'Will you marry me when I come back, Megan?' And she felt so happy she wanted to cry.

'Yes,' she said, although it wasn't necessary to say it because he knew by then how much she loved him; she had told him, over and over.

'A trick of fate,' he said. 'Meeting you just before I leave—why couldn't we have met a year ago?'

'I wasn't working on Johnny Fabian's show a year ago,' she pointed out, laughing and feeling a little light-headed. 'I was still at college.'

He frowned. 'At college . . . yes, you're so young, I keep forgetting.'

Her heart constricted. 'I like older men,' she pretended to tease, to cover her fear. He was thirty-five; the difference in age didn't honestly bother her but she had already sensed that it made Dev uneasy, especially when his friends made stupid, envious jokes about it.

'They'll say I'm cradle-snatching,' he said now, so he, too, was thinking about his friends.

'I'm hardly a child,' Megan said, wishing she was taller and looked older; but her build was against her. She was slight and fragile-looking; a tiny, pale girl to have such a heavy weight of hair and such great, wide-open eyes. She wasn't pretty, and found it puzzling that Dev should be attracted to anyone as unglamorous as herself when he must have plenty of pretty and glamorous women to choose from. It scared her, too, because it might be a passing fancy, a whim;

and what if he changed?

'You've been working for Fabian for six months, and that would age anybody!' Dev agreed, his tone dry because he didn't like Johnny, but then men rarely did. Johnny Fabian was a woman's man; his own sex resented him.

'I'm old enough to know what I want,' Megan said, then blurted out, 'Dev, couldn't I come with you?'

He stared, his face tight. 'Up the Amazon? Are you crazy?'

'Lots of women have been there, Dev!'

'On holiday trips in and out of the more populated region, maybe—but that is the whole point of this expedition: we're going to the largely unexplored region, and we're going to stay there for months on end. God knows what you could pick up—we've all had the most horrific courses of injections against the more common diseases rife out there, but then there are the snakes and the insects, any of which could give you a bite that would make you very ill indeed, if it didn't actually kill you. We can't inoculate you against snake bite or any of the microscopic things swimming in the river. We can't save you from the humidity or the sticky heat or the terrible rainy season, not to mention some of the more unpredictable human inhabitants.' He pushed her away to arm's length, still holding on to her, shaking her slightly. 'If I could take you, don't you think I'd have suggested it? It's impossible, Megan.'

'I'd take the risk,' she said eagerly.

'Megan, I couldn't concentrate on my job if I

had to keep worrying about you! I've visited South America before; not the Amazon, but other parts of the continent which have similar terrain. To some extent I'm ready for what I'll come up against. You wouldn't be. You've hardly been out of England before, have you?'

She lifted her chin, her big eyes defiant. 'Of course I have! I travelled all over Europe on a train two years ago! Some friends and I spent the whole summer vacation touring around. It was a cheap holiday, and great fun. People told us then that it was risky, but we came through without a scratch. We didn't run into anything we couldn't handle.'

Dev groaned. 'The Amazon basin isn't Europe! There are no roads, let alone trains. We'll be using the river; canoes, living in them for safety half the time. No, Megan, it's out of the question for you to come, but whenever I can I'll write, and I'll let you have a string of addresses and dates so that you can write to me and I can pick your letters up at intervals.'

'Oh, but Dev . . .' she began, and then the french windows behind them opened and his sister, Emma, confronted them.

'Dev, what on earth are you doing out here? There are a lot of people still wanting to talk to you.'

'Let them wait,' he said with his typical ruthless indifference to what other people wanted.

'Dev!' his sister protested. 'There are some very important people in there!'

'There's a very important person out here, too,' he said with wry amusement, deliberately encircing Megan with is arm.

His sister's pale eyes narrowed and she stiffened. Megan had only met her for the first time tonight, and she knew that Emma Stansfield hadn't really noticed her. Dev's sister looked oddly like him; the same colouring and features but in a more feminine mould, which yet had far more arrogance and pride of family than Dev had ever shown Megan. The Hursts were wealthy and had a long pedigree; they even had a remote connection with royalty some generations back. Emma had married one of her brother's oldest friends, Graham Stansfield, a member of the banking family; no doubt it had been viewed as a very suitable marriage when it took place, ten years ago, and from the look on Emma's elegant face now she was not going to see Megan as in any way suitable to marry into her family!

'Megan and I just got engaged,' Dev said. Megan wondered if it was her imagination that there was a ring of defiance in his tone.

'Engaged?' his sister repeated slowly, as if querying the word.

'There isn't time to get married before I leave, but we'll fix the date as soon as I'm back.' Dev was watching his sister, those grey eyes disturbingly chilly. Megan had seen that look on his face once or twice before, when someone angered him, and she shivered, hoping he would never turn that stare on her. 'Aren't you going to congratulate us, Emma?' he drawled, and there was something in his voice akin to a warning.

His sister's face tightened, her red mouth a thin

line. At last she said, 'Of course!' then added coldly, 'Congratulations.' She wasn't looking at her brother, though, or speaking to him; the word was drawled at Megan and it was dripping with sarcasm. Megan felt sick as it dawned on her that Dev's sister suspected her of ensnaring him. He was highly eligible, there was no denying that, and Megan hated the idea that people might think she was marrying him for his money or status. She felt Dev's body tighten; the fingers holding her waist curled, then released her.

'Megan, I'd like a word or two alone with my sister—why don't you go in and get us both a drink? I'll join you in a minute.'

Flushed and distressed, she gave a hasty nod, without saying anything, and hurried towards the open french windows, glad to get away. It should have dawned on her that Dev's family might not welcome her, but his proposal had come as a blinding surprise to her, she hadn't been expecting it, so she had not ever considered his family's reaction.

She closed the french window behind her, but in her haste she didn't click the lock home, and the window suddenly blew open again. Megan went back to shut it and heard Emma Stansfield's voice raised in cold mockery.

'You can't seriously intend to marry that plain little nobody!'

'Oh, but I do, and I shall expect all of you to be kind to her!' Dev's voice was angrily commanding, but his sister wasn't overawed.

'Why her, though? For heaven's sake, Dev, why

someone like that? She's so . . . so . . .' Emma
Stansfield paused and Megan heard her breathing,
then she said loudly, 'So ordinary!'

'That's why,' Dev said flatly, and Megan
flinched, her blue eyes wide in pain. Was that how
he saw her? As ordinary? A plain little nobody, his
sister had called her, and Dev hadn't argued with
that judgement; he had merely said be nice to
her—or else!

There was a silence outside on the terrace, as if
Emma Stansfield and her brother were staring at
each other and communicating without words,
then Dev spoke again in the same calm, quiet
voice.

'I want children, a family, a home, and she'll
give them to me.'

Emma's voice was different now, softer, almost
pleading. 'Dev, not all beautiful women are like
Gianna. You don't have to pick a boring little
mouse to get a loving wife! This girl won't fit in,
you know!'

'That's up to the family,' Dev said with hard
emphasis. 'If you make friends with her . . .'

'Make friends with her!' Emma repeated,
sounding outraged, and Megan very quietly closed
the window and stood there, fighting with tears.

She had known about Gianna Montesi, of
course; it had been much written about in the
Press, that affair. The gossip columns had really
gone to town on it, and when Megan was
researching Devlin Hurst before he appeared on
the Johnny Fabian show she had had to read her
way through acres of print on the subject. It had

happened a long time ago, though, she remembered, and, although Dev was frequently seen at parties or out at dinner with other women during the years following Gianna's sudden marriage to an American oilman, there had never been another 'big' affair, nothing that hit the headlines or seemed likely to end in a wedding.

Had Dev been deeply in love, and badly hurt? She bit her lip, closing her eyes in a spasm of jealousy.

From what Emma had said, he obviously had, and Gianna's rejection had left him determined never to fall for a woman of her kind again. Megan swallowed, the pain so intense that she had to clench her teeth not to cry out with it. She had been amazed that he showed such interest in her, hadn't she? Amazed and stupidly grateful, because a man like Devlin Hurst so much as looked twice at her! And all the time he had been picking her because she was just ordinary; a plain little nobody who would give him the children he wanted, make a home for him, be adoringly devoted all her life because he had chosen her!

'Oh, there you are, Megan! I was beginning to think you had gone home! What have you been up to?'

Johnny Fabian's light, amused voice broke in on her mood like a sudden blow, and she started, eyes wide in shock.

'Hey! Don't jump like that! What's up with you? Your nerves are in a hell of a state!' Johnny stood close to her, staring, while she fought to get herself under control again.

'You startled me, that's all.' Her voice wasn't quite steady, though, and Johnny's shrewd, dark eyes watched her curiously. 'Were you looking for me? What did you want?' Sometimes it worked to distract him with questions, and the last thing Megan wanted was to make Johnny curious, because he had the nose for secrets of a highly trained truffle-hound. That was what made his show so popular: Johnny found out things people wanted to keep hidden, and he loved to deflate the pompous, bring down the over-confident.

Of course, there were other reasons why his show was one of the top-rated chat shows on TV—and all of them began and ended with Johnny himself. He came from an extraordinary family; had a French grandmother and a Russian grandfather, an English mother and an American father; spoke six languages fluently and could get by in heaven knew how many others, and added to his undoubted brains an unfair amount of good looks and charm. Women couldn't resist him when he gave one of his sudden, wicked smiles and made one of his famous little gestures—pushed back his thick, curly auburn hair, looked sideways with narrowed eyes, gave one of his wry, resigned shrugs. They were such practised movements, but they never failed to gain their effect. Johnny could do no wrong in the eyes of his adoring fans. Anyone who wasn't a fan usually loathed him, but that didn't bother Johnny. He knew which side his bread was buttered, and he ignored his enemies, concentrating on pleasing his fans.

'I've been talking to someone interesting, that's

all, and I wondered if he might do for the show so I was going to ask you to check him out some time next week, only I couldn't find you, could I? So I wondered where you could have got to . . .' His voice faded as the french windows opened and Dev walked into the house. Dev paused, seeing Megan, then realised that she was with Johnny and walked on, his brows dark.

Johnny caught that look and stared at Megan, whistling softly. She had kept quiet about her dates with Dev since he'd appeared on the show. She hadn't wanted any gossip about them and had not wanted to be teased, or questioned, either.

'Don't tell me you were with him?' Johnny asked incredulously. 'Are you out of your mind, honey? The two of you don't have a thing in common and, anyway, he's off up the Amazon in a couple of days. I thought you had more sense.'

Megan's face was white and stiff, but she tried to sound normal. 'Who was it you wanted me to check out?'

'And you know it isn't wise to get involved with any of our guests; it can cause all sorts of complications, and it's a habit I don't encourage.'

'I don't make a habit of it!'

'Glad to hear it,' Johnny said, still watching her out of those shrewd, dark, beautiful eyes. 'Megan . . . Meggy . . . I don't want you to get hurt!'

'I'm in no danger of getting hurt,' she said, crossing her fingers behind her back in the age-old gesture of protection, and Johnny shrugged, grimacing.

'OK, honey, if you say so! Mark Bond.'

She stared blankly. 'Sorry?' Sometimes Johnny's gnomic muttering baffled her.

'The possible guest I want you to check out. Mark Bond.'

The name was totally unknown to her. 'Who is he?' Megan moved to where she could see most of the other guests in the enormous room in which the party was being held. Her blue eyes flicked from face to face, but she couldn't guess which of them had caught Johnny's attention.

'By the fireplace,' directed Johnny, and Megan's eyes moved sideways to where a man in an evening suit was leaning against the lovely Georgian fireplace.

'Who is he?' He wasn't elegant, in spite of his well-cut clothes; the body underneath them was far too muscled; shoulders broad, chest deep, legs long, it was the body of an athlete or a wrestler.

'I gather he's a sculptor.'

'Sculptor?' Megan stared even harder. 'Sure he isn't pulling your leg? If you'd said all-in wrestler, I'd have believed you.'

Johnny grinned. 'That's why I want you to check him out. He may be selling me a line, but if he's on the level he would be fun to have on the show. He's very funny about his work. Doesn't take it, or himself, too seriously. Might be interesting to have him bring whatever he's currently working on . . . he could maybe . . . what's the operative word, sculpt? . . . on the show. What do you think?'

'Sounds interesting, so long as he doesn't do massive figures, like Henry Moore! Have you told

Fanny?'

'It's my show!' Johnny was quick to take offence if he thought you took more notice of the producer's opinion than his own.

'Of course, Johnny,' soothed Megan at once. 'I just wondered what she thought. She collects garden statuary, doesn't she? I wondered if Mark Bond was in that line, that's all.'

Distracted, Johnny said, 'I'd forgotten Fanny and her garden statues. Yes, I must have a word with her, but meanwhile go and chat Mark Bond up, would you? Ask him to lunch, see if you can get into his studio or whatever. Get a look at his stuff and ring round the various dealers to get an idea how good he is—or isn't, as the case may be!'

'OK,' Megan said, watching the stranger on the other side of the room. She was rather grateful for the excuse to keep out of Dev's way; she needed time to think, and a chat with Mark Bond might be the perfect cover. Megan couldn't believe that Johnny was serious about this, though. He often met people at parties whom he thought might make good guests, only to change his mind in the morning when he was sober, but as far as Megan could judge he didn't appear to be drunk tonight.

'Not yet!' Johnny said, glancing at his watch. 'My car should be here by now, shouldn't it?'

'I'll go and see if it has arrived.' Johnny's chauffeur-driven limousine always arrived to whisk him away in good time so that if he wanted an excuse for leaving a party one was at hand; but the chauffeur just waited outside, knowing that if Johnny was enjoying himself he wouldn't want to go back to his luxurious but empty flat. Unless Johnny took someone home with him, of course. That had been known to happen! Johnny usually had a problem keeping women away, rather than attracting them, and that was why Johnny lived alone, in fact. There had always been too many women eager to vie for his attention; he was spoilt and hard to please.

'Aren't you enjoying yourself, Johnny?' Megan asked him with a sympathetic little smile.

'This isn't the greatest party in the world, is it?' he replied discontentedly. He caught her hand. 'Why don't you and me go and have a late, late supper together somewhere with a better atmosphere than this?

She gave him an indulgent smile. 'Not tonight, Johnny, thanks.' Gently disentangling herself, she hurried off to see if his car had arrived, and only then did she realise that Dev was watching them, his face coldly expressionless. Megan's eyes met his briefly, then she looked away because she could not face him just yet. She did not know what to do. She was deeply in love with Dev, but whatever his reasons for proposing to her she no longer believed that he was in love with her, not now that she had heard him discussing her with his sister in that cool, distant fashion. That hadn't been the voice of a man in love, had it? She had to think long and hard. Wouldn't it be madness to get engaged to him, knowing why he really wanted to marry her? Yet if she told him she had changed her mind, if she said goodbye and never saw him again, could she bear that, either?

The alternatives facing her were equally unbearable, and Megan's heart ached as she went to find Johnny's chauffeur.

The limousine was parked under the lime trees lining the long drive up to Dev's beautiful family home. The chauffeur was sitting inside, smoking; Megan saw the glowing red tip of a cigar, saw him flick ash, then start the engine as he noticed her on the stone steps under the portico of the house, waving to him.

She went back into the house as the long, black car smoothly slid up the drive to wait right outside for Johnny.

The party was as noisy as ever, the guests a swirl of colour and noise under the beautiful swags of crystal chandeliers. Megan stood in the doorway looking around for Johnny, and took a moment to locate him, only to have her nerves jump in alarm when she saw him with Dev. Their faces were tight and angry; they faced each other like duellists. Megan took a deep breath and hurried over. What had Johnny been saying, for God's sake, to make Dev look like that?

'Your car's here!' she said quickly as they both looked round at her.

Johnny nodded, then gave Dev a hard look. 'I hope you got the message!' he said, took Megan's arm and pulled her away with him, saying, 'Now, go and chat up Mark Bond, and stay away from Hurst after this.'

'Johnny, what did you say to him? Her voice was angry and upset, but he was too pleased with himself to care, grinning at her in satisfaction.

'I just told him that you were my property; that should keep him at arm's length.'

'Johnny!' She was appalled, going red then white. 'How could you? Oh, how could you?'

CHAPTER TWO

MEGAN might have known that it would be useless to reproach Johnny, who was convinced he knew best about everything. He patted her shoulder soothingly.

'You'll thank me for it before too long. After all, he'll be gone soon, and a year is a lifetime. Believe me—I know.' Johnny had never kept up a relationship that long; no doubt he did think a year was a lifetime, but Megan didn't want the sort of self-centred life Johnny led. It would be far too lonely. He didn't care for anyone but himself. He might be rich and famous, and some people might envy or admire his way of life, but she thought it was sad. She often felt sorry for Johnny, but not at the moment. She was blazingly angry with him, and it showed in her fierce blue eyes.

'That's just it—you don't know! You're not me, and you had no business interfering in my life! Don't ever do it again!'

Johnny looked amazed. She had never spoken to him like that before; few people ever did. He was too important, and Megan, like everybody else, usually took care not to offend or annoy him, but even at the risk of losing her job she wasn't going to let him come between her and Dev.

She glared at him, then turned on her heel and looked around for Dev, to tell him not to take any notice of Johnny. Dev was by the door, but he wasn't alone. His sister was talking vehemently to him, and Megan couldn't face Emma Stansfield again, so reluctantly she went over to talk to Mark Bond. He was talking to one of the camera crew going to South America with Dev, who recognised Megan with a grin, putting a lazy arm around her. 'Hi, Meggy, how are you?' He was slightly tipsy, but very cheerful, and she smiled back at his thin, lively face.

'I'm fine, how are you, Charlie?'

'Fine; can't wait to get on that plane.' His hazel eyes shone with enthusiasm. Charlie had once worked on the Fabian show, for a few weeks, and Megan had got to know him then. He had confided to her that he hated studio work, and longed to get into outside broadcasting, or location work in films. He was thrilled to have got this job with Dev.

'I bet you can't!' she teased, amused. 'You're going to have the time of your life for the next year! Just steer clear of snakes and poisonous insects.'

'I like snakes,' he said seriously. 'Used to keep them when I was a kid; I had half a dozen at one time until my mother got hysterical and made me get rid of them all.'

'I once did a study of Medusa,' said Mark Bond thoughtfully, staring at Megan. 'I had quite a job talking my model into holding a perfectly harmless grass snake; she wouldn't be convinced that it wouldn't give her a lethal bite!'

'Most people are like that; my mother, for one,' said Charlie, then stopped, noticing the obvious way the other man was watching Megan, and said, 'Bad-mannered of me; I didn't introduce you—Megan, this is Mark Bond, the sculptor. Mark, this is Megan Carr, one of the researchers, on the Fabian show.'

Mark Bond held out his hand, smiling. He had a leonine head; thick, silvery blond hair swept back from a distinct widow's peak, narrowed blue eyes, a very strongly moulded face.

'Hello—oddly enough, I was talking to Johnny Fabian himself earlier.'

She smiled back. 'Really?' She didn't tell him that Johnny had mentioned him; it wouldn't do to raise his hopes in case Johnny changed his mind about having him on the show. 'Charlie said you were a sculptor; what sort of work do you do?'

He looked impatient, running a wiry hand through his smooth, pale hair. 'People will ask that, and I never know what to say. I sculpt in stone and wood . . .'

'Wood?' she queried, and he nodded.

'You can call it wood-carving, if you prefer, but, although the techniques are different, the aim is the same. You're bringing out of the material whatever you see in it. Before you ever touch it you start to see the hidden shape inside; I often buy a block of stone or a piece of wood because I want to create what I think I can see in it.'

'Do you have a buyer in mind before you start work, or do you sculpt something and just hope to sell it when it's finished?'

'Well, both. If someone offers me a commission to do some specific piece of work I'll do that, if it appeals to me—but if not, I just work on whatever occurs to me.'

'I'd love to see some of your work,' Megan said, aware of Charlie's watching eyes and the amusement in them. Charlie probably guessed that Johnny had asked her to check out Mark Bond, and it made her self-conscious to have him watching her.

She frowned at him sideways, and he got the message, saying to Mark, 'Will you excuse me? I've just spotted a terrific blonde who looks as if she needs some friendly company.' Grinning at Megan, he added, 'I'll leave you in our Meggy's capable hands; nice to have met you, Mark.'

Mark cheerfully said, 'Have a good trip up the Amazon! I wish I was going with you.'

Charlie laughed and pushed his way into the chatting throng while Megan smiled at Mark Bond.

'Would you really like to go up the Amazon?'

'Love to, but I've never managed to clear enough space in my life. Time is the big problem, isn't it?'

'I hope you can find time to let me see some of your work, at least!' she smiled, feeling devious and not too happy about it, but Mark looked pleased.

'Any day you like; it will be a pleasure. I never have any difficulty talking about my work. In fact, you'll have to stop me when I start boring you.'

'I'm sure you won't,' said Megan, mentally crossing her fingers behind her back. She had been bored out of her skull for the sake of the programme more times than she could remember; she thought she would survive another hour or two of it. It all depended how good a sculptor he was, of course!

'Tomorrow?' he said, and, knowing Johnny was capable of expecting her to have a portfolio on him by dawn tomorrow, she nodded.

'Wonderful.' From the look in his eyes, she realised that he must think she was using an interest in his sculpture as an excuse for meeting him again, which was a nuisance, but that couldn't be helped. Anyway, he didn't look the type to make a heavy pass right away.

A few minutes later, they were joined by another friend of the Hursts, a well-known politician who wanted to talk to Mark about having himself immortalised in stone. 'A bust,' he elaborated. 'Not my idea, of course; it was suggested by my constituency people.'

Megan met Mark's wry glance and smiled a trifle mischievously. 'Will you excuse me? I've just seen someone I must say hello to . . .'

Mark gave her a pleading look, but she abandoned him to his fate. At least he would get a commission out of it, and she had to find Dev!

While she was talking to Mark, she had occasionally glanced towards Dev, to check that he was still with Emma, but when she looked for him now both he and Emma had gone. Megan soon saw Emma, talking to a little group of people, but

Dev wasn't one of them.

She began to hunt through the ground-floor rooms of the lovely old house without catching sight of him anywhere. People kept trying to talk to her; friends of the Hursts, of course, mostly from an easily recognisable tribe, glossy and assured. The people she worked with had another sort of glamour, but the men and women whom she was meeting tonight had that patronising look, meant to convey their tolerant contempt for her world, for television and all who worked for it; in particular the Fabian show.

She smiled indifferently; it was all water off a duck's back, especially as she knew that they would jump at an invitation to appear on the show.

That was something else her job was all about, recognising the difference between what people said and what they really thought. She would hate to become cynical, but it was hard not to be, at times.

She was in the hall when she heard Dev's name and paused to eavesdrop shamelessly on two guests. 'I haven't seen him all evening, I suppose he actually came to his own party?' one man said, laughing.

'Oh, yes, he's around. I saw him go into the library a while ago,' said the other.

Her long, pale oyster silk skirts rustling, Megan opened the double oak doors of the library, then paused on the threshold of the long room in some surprise because the room was in darkness. Dev couldn't be in here, after all! she thought, sighing, and then his voice spoke harshly from the other side of the room.

'Who's that?'

'Dev?'

There was a silence, then he said in the same grating tone, 'Go back to the party, Megan; go back to Fabian.'

Closing the door, she went towards him, talking hurriedly so that he shouldn't stop her. 'Dev, you mustn't take any notice of what Johnny said! He thought he was protecting me from getting hurt; he doesn't think I should get engaged until I know you better. He meant well, but it was all nonsense. You know there isn't anything between me and Johnny!'

Again silence, then a movement as he leaned over and switched on a silk table-lamp, throwing a warm, roseate glow on to the muted gleam of her oyster silk dress with its full skirts and tight waist.

She blinked in the sudden brightness; seeing him through her lashes in a golden auriole. He looked so unfamiliar; hard and remote. So was his voice. 'Perhaps he was right, all the same. I had no business blurting out a proposal at the last minute; giving you no time to think, taking you by surprise.' The harshness was gone, but the chill in his voice was somehow worse.

She was getting used to the light; she looked at his strong, grim face and hesitated, remembering that overheard talk between him and his sister. Did he love her, or had he proposed cold-bloodedly because she would be satisfied with having his children and making him a home, whereas more beautiful women might want more?

Dev looked back at her, his brows lifting at her silence, and her heart seemed to turn over inside her. It was shameful to admit it; she knew she should hate herself, but she couldn't help loving him and she didn't care whether he loved her or not, she wanted him too much to care why he had chosen her. It was enough that he had.

She knelt down beside his wing armchair while he watched her in an unreadable silence.

'You certainly took me by surprise,' she said, smiling shakily at him. 'But I didn't need any time to think. I love you, and I want to be your wife more than anything in the world.'

He didn't move, staring at her, and she wished she knew what he was thinking, then she was glad that she didn't. Dev looked oddly lonely in here, in these shadows; he needed her, whether he loved her or not. People always said that you liked people who liked you—didn't that apply to love, too?

'Megan, it wouldn't work,' he said heavily, his hands gripping the arms of the leather-upholstered chair.

'Oh, Dev,' she whispered, and put her cheek against the nearest hand, closing her eyes and letting the peace of his closeness flow into her.

He stiffened and for an instant she thought he would snatch his hand away, then his other hand moved, she felt his fingers on her hair, stroking and winnowing. Pleasure held her captive, she hardly breathed as his hand slid under her hair, caressed her bare nape, making her whole body weak with the erotic glide of his fingertips.

After a few moments, he said flatly, 'Marriage is a big step, especially as I'm going away for so long. We won't get engaged, Megan . . .'

'But . . .' she began and he cut in tersely,

'No! You may change your mind once I've gone, for a start!'

'I won't!'

'You can't possibly know that, Megan. At the moment you may think you love me . . .'

'I don't think I do. I know I do. How young do you think I am? I'm not a child, Dev. I'm an adult woman and I know what I want.'

He laughed shortly, that hand closing on her throat, lifting her face towards him. 'Do you?' His voice was lower, deeper; sending a long shudder down her spine. One thing had always been undeniable: the physical drag between them, a sensual attraction she read in Dev's eyes now, darkening his gaze, dilating his pupils.

He bent very slowly, still watching her until the moment when his mouth caught hers. Megan's eyes closed and her lips parted, thirsting for the taste of his kiss. Dev's arms went round her, tightened, pulling her up on to his lap, her body yielding warmly. Everything she was flowed out to him in that kiss; she put her arms around him and held him close to her. This was how it would feel to hold his child, she thought suddenly, and she ached to have Dev's child, to hold it in her arms. It was a thought that had never occurred to her before in her life; her whole being seemed to be shaken up and thrown about as if in a kaleidoscope, coming down in an entirely new pattern.

She had just told him that she knew what she wanted, but until now she really hadn't known. She knew now; she understood herself and life better than she ever had before.

Her long, cloudy hair surrounded them both, making a tent for them in which they kissed, while Dev's hands explored downwards, warm on the oyster silk, far warmer on her bare skin, making her draw a sharp breath and shudder, although not with cold—on the contrary, it was the burning heat between them that made her shake.

Dev might not be in love with her, but she had no doubts abut his desire for her. That side of their marriage would work, anyway!

He suddenly broke off the kiss, breathing roughly as he lifted his head. His face was darkly flushed, his eyes smouldering. 'We'd better stop now, while we can,' he murmured thickly, and she laughed shakily, very flushed.

Dev looked at her with a crooked smile. 'A pity we didn't meet a year ago; we could have been married by now!'

She was so moved she couldn't hold his gaze; she looked down, trembling.

She felt him watching her for a moment, then he said quietly, 'If you change your mind you'll write and tell me honestly? We won't get engaged, Megan; not yet, not until I come back. I don't want to burden you with guilt if you meet someone else while I'm away.'

'I won't,' she said quickly, but Dev just shook his head ruefully.

'Promise me!' he insisted.

She gazed at him, wondering if he was using Johnny's interference as an excuse for doing what he really wanted to do—back out of his proposal? Had he asked her to marry him on the spur of the moment, only to realise when he talked to his sister that it would be a mistake to marry a girl his family thought of as a 'plain little nobody'?

'If I ever do meet anyone, I'll tell you,' she said at last, and he gave an audible sigh. Was that relief or regret? she wondered, her disturbed blue eyes hunting over his face for clues to his true feelings, but Devlin Hurst was a past master at hiding his thoughts and emotions. He looked back at her, his features masked and unreadable.

Then they heard the raised voices outside the double doors, and froze, turning to look in alarm across the room, but the doors didn't open, the voices moved further off. Dev laughed wryly.

'This isn't the time or place, is it?' He kissed her hair, his lips moving softly. 'Sexy hair! In Victorian times, men used to wear a lock of their true love's hair around their necks in a locket.'

Megan sat up a little and leaned over to pick up a pair of scissors from the desk; offering them to him with a sideways little smile. 'Take your pick.'

It was half a joke, but Dev took the scissors slowly and ran his fingers into her hair, staring at it, before snipping off some long, curling strands. He took his wallet out of his inside jacket pocket and slid the lock of hair into it. Megan watched him, entranced; the action had been mesmeric, oddly ritualistic.

She could almost believe Dev loved her, and that gave her the courage to ask, 'Can't I come and see you off at Heathrow?' Dev had said firmly that he did not want her to be there to wave goodbye, but she thought he might weaken if she asked him now.

He looked down at her and shook his head, though. 'No, Megan! I told you—I'd hate saying goodbye in front of half the world, especially with the Press there. I'm going to be very busy from now until we leave, so we'll say goodbye tonight.'

Megan went pale, her body wincing. 'Can't we see each other again one more time?' She hadn't been expecting this and was not prepared for it.

'No,' he said, and although she pleaded for some time he would not give in; he had made up his mind and would not budge. Megan looked at him helplessly. Why on earth had she fallen in love with someone so immovable?

Next day, she got to Mark Bond's studio on time but there was no answer when she rang the bell. She was about to leave when she saw him jogging along the road towards her. He waved, and she waved back, smiling.

'Hi!' he said, a little breathless. 'Am I late? Sorry, I thought I'd be back by now, but I saw someone I know and had to stop and chat.' He was wearing a plum-coloured tracksuit and matching track shoes, and managed to make the outfit look a million dollars.

'That's OK, I haven't been here long!' said Megan, as he opened the front door and waved her through. 'Do you always jog in the mornings?'

'Usually. You need muscles in my job.'

'I suppose you would!' agreed Megan, thinking of some of the vast statues she had seen.

'While I'm showering and changing, why don't you make us some coffee?' Mark said, gesturing to door. 'Kitchen's through there. I won't be long.' He vanished into another room and Megan wryly went into the galley-style kitchen; impressed by the very well-thought-out layout with everything within easy reach. No doubt he had had a first-class kitchen design firm to install the handsome cream and maroon fittings. She made the coffee and stood for a moment looking out of the window at a long, lawned garden which led down to the river Thames. She could just glimpse the steely shine of water through willows. Mark Bond must be successful to afford this flat in this house; it was a very desirable residential neighbourhood.

What was Dev doing this morning? she wondered, sighing. He was busy, of course, getting ready for that year-long trip, but surely he could have made time to see her? Perhaps he would ring tonight? Talking to him for a few minutes would be better than nothing! Lost in thought, she gave a choked gasp as warm, silky fur brushed her leg.

'Don't you like cats?'

Laughing, she looked round at Mark Bond, who was now wearing a conventional white shirt and smooth grey trousers.

'Yes, but I wasn't expecting one just then!' She bent down to stroke the delicate little Siamese with the strange blue eyes, but it undulated away from her hand and stalked off, offended, tail in the air.

Megan made a face and Mark Bond laughed, then inhaled the scent of the coffee.

'Do I need this! Shall we take it through into the studio?' He picked up the tray and Megan followed him across the corridor into a long, spacious, light-filled room with the end wall entirely made of glass through which she saw the same view she had seen from the kitchen: grass and trees and distant river.

'Sit here,' Mark said, laying down the tray on the floor. He curled up next to it and began pouring coffee. Megan hesitated beside the only chair; a Victorian balloon-backed chair covered in deep red velvet. Mark gave her a grin. 'Go on, sit down. I keep that for visitors. My grandmother gave it to me; she swore it had once belonged to Dante Gabriel Rossetti, but I don't believe a word of it.'

Megan sat down, took the cup he held out to her. 'It's a romantic thought, though, isn't it?'

He studied her. 'Ah, you're romantic, are you?'

She flushed. 'And you're not?'

'I keep it, so maybe I am,' he mocked, pulling a tray full of large sheets of cartridge paper towards him. Picking out a sheet, he began sketching, his eyes on Megan. 'You don't mind, do you? I feel ill at ease with idle fingers.'

Megan wasn't sure she didn't mind, but didn't like to object, so to cover her uneasiness she looked around at the high-ceilinged, white-walled, rectangular room. There were several sheet-draped objects in it; she tried to guess what they were. That one must be a woman, she decided—

what other shape had those particular curves? Had he draped them to hide them from her?

'Those sheets look like veils,' she said. 'They're making me curious about what's underneath.'

He grinned. 'Isn't that always the way with veils? I sometimes think women should never have stopped wearing them.'

Megan laughed. 'I'm glad they did! How boring, going around in a veil all day.' She watched his deft fingers and wondered what the sketch of her would be like; she couldn't remember anyone ever drawing her before.

'Want to see?' He offered the sheet of paper to her and she stared at the sketch, taken aback by it. 'Well? What do you think?' he asked, and she looked at him uncertainly.

'It's very good.' Yet it was alarming, too. She felt he had shown her things about herself she hadn't known; it was not the Megan Carr she knew, and yet she had to recognise the truth of it, and that was disturbing.

There was an uncovered and powerful clay head on a turntable nearby, so to cover her uneasiness she looked at that. She didn't recognise the sitter but the force of the thing hit you from across the room; it was as dominating as any living human being, and it made her eager to see more of his work.

'I am going to see your work, aren't I?' she asked, as she finished her coffee, and Mark Bond laughed.

'That's why you're here!'

She smiled uncertainly, wondering if he guessed

the reason behind her sudden fascination with his work.

'Give me a hand with these sheets,' Mark said, rising, and she got to her feet to help him. He looked down at her, his eyes very bright and intent, and Megan stared into them in faint bewilderment. Why was he looking at her like that? She soon found out. He bent and kissed her, taking her by surprise before she could move away. His lips were warm and coaxing, and she might have enjoyed the experience if she hadn't been in love with another man. Stiffening, she pushed him away, and he lifted his head to look down into her eyes in a long, searching stare.

'Whoops!'

That wry exclamation threw Megan. 'What?'

'In case you didn't notice, I just made one hell of a mistake,' he drily said. 'Obviously, I put two and two together and made it five. I thought you invited yourself here because you fancied me.'

She flushed. 'Oh!'

'Which you clearly don't!'

Megan looked unhappily at him; she had been afraid that he would jump to some such conclusion!

'OK, no need to look tragic,' he drawled, mouth crooked. 'So if it wasn't my fatal charm that brought you here, what was it? You scarcely seem to be a sculpture buff. I don't think you know anything about sculpture.'

She sighed. 'I'm not, no! I am interested in it, that is—really! But . . . well, Johnny asked me to check you out, you see. It's possible he might ask you on the show, but first . . .'

'Fabian told you to chat me up?' he interrupted, brows heavy. 'Does he always send you to flirt with possible guests for his show?'

Hot, angry colour ran up her face. 'I'm one of his researchers. It doesn't make me part of the deal, Mr Bond, and Johnny doesn't require me to flirt with anyone.' She pushed past him and headed for the door. 'Forget it. Thank you for your time.'

He caught up with her before she had finished speaking. 'Megan! I'm sorry! That was damned rude of me. No excuses, but I suppose I found it hard to take the fact that you hadn't come round just because you liked me.'

'That sounds remarkably like an excuse to me!' she said, but already softening, because Mark had a charm she couldn't help responding to; his smile was that of a naughty little boy: guilty, yet still hoping that he would be forgiven. He probably always was! She shook her head at him.' I should go now while I'm ahead!'

'Please stay!' he coaxed. 'Can't we start again?'

She could hardly refuse, so she accepted the hand he held out. 'Friends?' he asked, and she laughed and shrugged.

'Friends.'

'Good. Now, let's get the drapes off these things.'

Of course, it wasn't enough that he should be good at his work, or respected by the art world—he had to be able to talk if he was to appear on the show, and Megan listened intently as Mark showed her the sculptures in the studio. She had done some homework on him before she came and knew that he had sold pieces to several cities for public display, but the statues in the studio at present were all privately commissioned.

'I'd like to see one of your bigger statues,' she said thoughtfully.

'There's a vast shopping mall in North London which has one of my biggest pieces. The central hall of the mall has a fountain; they asked me to sculpt Neptune but I did something a little less obvious: sea-horses, fifteen-foot-high sea-horses thundering along in a cloud of spray—that's the fountain, not me, of course.'

'It sounds wonderful,' she said, watching his face intently; it was so alive, so vibrant, especially when his eyes glowed like that. Yes, he could certainly talk well, on his own subject.

'I have to go there tonight, to one of those city hall dinners. Back-patting affairs! You know, Councillor this and my Lord Mayor that, all telling each other how wonderful they are! I'm invited for the official unveiling of my sea-horses.' He suddenly stopped, looking at her with his head to one side. 'Why don't you come along? My invitation card says bring a guest and I wasn't planning to . . . but you could see the fountain and it might be fun.'

Megan hesitated; half drawn to the idea because she would like to see the magical sea-horses he talked of with so much excitement, and half reluctant to go anywhere in case Dev rang her.

But she knew, in her heart of hearts, that he wouldn't. Dev had made it crystal-clear that he would be too busy to see her; he had virtually cut her off and she was only fooling herself if she hoped to hear from him again before he left the country. Maybe in a couple of months she would get a postcard from some remote little town on the Amazon. Oh, Dev had promised to write as often as he could, and he might write now and then, in between more vital jobs, or when he had nothing else to do, but he was obsessed with this project of his, and Dev was a ruthlessly committed man. Once he was out there he would often be out of touch with civilisation for weeks on end. He might as well be going to the moon.

If she stayed at home she would brood over Dev all evening—perhaps it would be wiser to go out?

'Thank you, I'd love to see your sea-horses!' she said, and saw from Mark's face that he was surprised, had not expected her to accept.

That evening, while she was waiting for Mark to pick her up, she rang Dev, but his voice was recorded; she could only talk to his answering machine; which she was tempted to do, pouring out her feelings as she heard his living, yet already distant voice. Of course, she didn't; she didn't even leave a message, she silently hung up. It seemed an omen, especially when it began to rain. She sat by the window, in the half-light, listening to the hypnotic sound of water washing down the glass, swishing along the gutters in the street, drumming on roofs and cars. She was haunted by the knowledge that Dev was somewhere in the city and within reach, yet had already said goodbye to her.

She didn't understand him. If she could, she would spend every precious minute of these last few days with him—why didn't he want that? Did he really love her? A fierce stab of pain inside her made her want to curl up in a foetus-like ball of misery. Dev was a strange country whose maps she could not read, and in which she was always lost.

The doorbell buzzed; it was Mark, a few minutes early and very striking in formal dark evening clothes.

He smiled down at her, his brows lifting as he whistled admiration. 'You're looking very special tonight! I love that dress.'

'Thank you.' Megan was pleased with his reaction; she liked the dress too; it was one of her favourites, not new, but one in which she always felt wonderful because she knew it suited her. The rich, gentian blue of the taffeta brought out the colour of her eyes, and the tight waist and low bodice gave her figure more impact. She had altered her hairstyle, brushed back her black hair and pinned it up with diamanté stars so that it glittered and swished around her face when she turned her head.

'We make a great pair,' Mark said, taking her hand and drawing it through his arm on the way out to his car. 'Now, you're going to enjoy yourself tonight, and that's official.'

She laughed. 'Yes, sir, certainly, sir.'

'You aren't going to be bored, and if you go to sleep during the speeches I'll kick you under the table, and you'll do the same for me, which could be vital, as I'm one of the speakers and if it's me making the speech when I fall asleep someone might notice.'

'Unless they're all asleep, too?' she suggested, and he nodded as he started the engine.

'Knowing the power of my oratory, that is more than likely.'

'What do I do then?'

'Just let us all sleep, OK?'

In fact, he made a brilliant speech, funny and fascinating. Megan was very impressed; there was no doubt that he would be a big hit on the Fabian show. He was a big hit with the audience that night—and a big hit with Megan. She was just as struck by his incredible fountain; the horses took your breath away as they seemed to thunder towards you through the flying spray. An imaginative local council had lined the edge of the pool with water fern and water lilies. It gave the rather stark, windy mall a beautiful and tranquil centre, as Megan told Mark while he was driving her back to her flat.

'An improvement on some places I've seen,' he agreed, his eyes on the almost empty road. It was almost midnight, still raining, and most people seemed to be staying at home. Megan yawned convulsively.

'Tired?' said Mark, shooting her a glance. 'Never mind, we're nearly at your place.'

That was when the car began jerking and coughing, and Mark sat up, swearing. 'Oh, hell!'

'What's wrong?' Megan asked anxiously.

He slowly drew into the side of the road and

then stopped. Turning to look ruefully at her, he said, 'I'm out of petrol.' He watched her mouth open, then curve into amusement. 'Don't laugh, damn you! Unless a taxi happens by, you're going to have to walk home from here in this rain!'

She peered out and recognised the street. 'It's only a block from where I live, don't worry.' She huddled inside her short black velvet evening jacket, wryly realising that her clothes were going to get soaked.

'Could I use your phone to ring for a taxi?' Mark said. 'I'll have to leave my car here and come back for it tomorrow.'

'Of course.'

They ran through the rainy street, and laughing and breathless, almost fell into her flat, both of them dripping wet; their hair plastered to their heads and their clothes damp.

'The phone's in the sitting-room,' said Megan. 'Take your jacket off and dry it in front of the electric fire while you wait for the taxi. I'll make us some hot chocolate.'

'Mmm, you're an angel.' Mark stripped off his jacket while she switched on the fire, then she went to find him a towel for his hair, put on the milk for the chocolate and took off her wet dress, replacing it with a loose purple caftan. She had to hurry before the milk boiled over.

When she carried the mugs of hot chocolate into the sitting-room she found Mark sitting on the floor in front of the electric fire, listening to a jazz record and glancing through a glossy book about Renoir which someone had once given Megan for

Christmas.

'I hope you don't mind; I've made myself at home,' he said, giving her an impish grin. 'The taxi won't get here for twenty minutes. They said they were very busy tonight because of the rain.'

'No problem. So you like jazz, too?' Megan handed him his mug of chocolate, and curled up on the floor next to him, her own mug clasped between her cold hands.

'Love it! You must come and hear my collection some time . . .' The sudden clangour of the doorbell stopped him mid-sentence and his brows rose. 'Who can that be at this time of night?'

Megan had turned pink and was already on her feet. She didn't answer, but Mark's eyes narrowed at the look in her face as she rushed to the door, entirely forgetting him.

She ran, because she was afraid that if she didn't get there fast Dev would go again. She knew it was Dev, who else could it be at this hour?

He stood there in a short black leather jacket, the collar turned up, his hair darkened with rain, smiling at her.

'I was driving past when I saw your light come on and I thought I'd drop in to . . .' His voice died away as his eyes moved past her to the open door of the sitting-room through which he had a clear view of Mark in his shirt-sleeves, sprawled on the carpet by the fire, sipping his hot chocolate.

Slowly Dev looked back at Megan in her loose caftan, her hair tousled and fluffy where she had dried it with a towel hurriedly without afterwards running a comb through it.

She went scarlet as she suddenly realised what he was thinking. 'Dev, I . . . we've been . . .' she stammered, so upset she couldn't get out a sensible explanation.

'Sorry to have interrupted your cosy evening,' Dev said curtly before she could pull herself together, then he turned on his heel and strode off too fast for her to have a chance of catching up with him.

CHAPTER THREE

SHE tried to get in touch with him at his flat later, but there was only the answering machine at home; she left a husky message but Dev did not ring back. She didn't sleep, and went in to work heavy-eyed and unable to concentrate.

'What's the matter with you?' Johnny asked. 'Coming down with something nasty? Don't come near me, I don't want it.'

He wouldn't catch it, she thought. Johnny was immune to love; had he ever been a victim or had he been born immune?

'In fact, you'd better go home to bed and stay there,' he said from a safe distance. 'And don't come back until you're over whatever it is . . .'

She went home via Dev's flat, but he didn't come to the door when she rang the bell, and there was no sign of his car in the usual space. She put a note through the letterbox, explaining why Mark had been with her in her flat the night before, and asking him to call her. When he hadn't rung by lunch time, she tried again to ring him, but this time there wasn't even an answering maching. All she got was the steady whine of a disconnected phone. Dev had had his phone cut off.

Feverish and desperate, she paced the floor, watching the clock inexorably tick through the hours until Dev went. Surely he wouldn't go without seeing her? He must have got her messages. He must know now why Mark was at her flat at that hour, and he would realise how unhappy this misunderstanding had made her. He couldn't just fly away for a whole year without telling her he believed her, he knew the truth?

For a second night she went without sleep; even though she tried to relax in bed she couldn't, her brain was too active and she was too miserable.

Dawn found her white and shivering, almost hallucinating because she had had no sleep for two days. There was only one chance left, she thought, looking at her watch for the hundredth time. She had to go to Heathrow. Dev had insisted that he didn't want her there; there would be photographers and reporters there to see the team off, and Dev didn't want her involved in any of the publicity ballyhoo.

The situation had changed, though. She couldn't let him go without seeing him, even if only for a moment. She had to be sure that he knew he had jumped to the wrong conclusion when he saw Mark in her flat. Dev must not go off to South America without knowing the truth.

When she reached the airport she parked in the short-term car park and walked to the terminal building, but just as she got to the check-in desk she saw Dev and the rest of the team walking through the control barrier on the way to the departure lounge.

Running, she called his name; the others went on but he stopped and looked round. Megan waved, calling again, 'Dev!'

His cold grey eyes briefly met hers, then he
walked on, out of sight. She skidded to a halt,
feeling sick. He had gone. She couldn't believe
it; Dev had seen her and he had known very well
why she was here, but he had turned his back on
her and walked away.

Slowly she walked back to retrieve her car and
drove back into London, without really being
aware of what she was doing, acting like an
automaton. She was trapped inside a nightmare.
Lack of sleep, emotional stress, fever and weariness made the world seem totally unreal to her.
She kept moving because he couldn't think of
anything else to do. She could not break down in
the airport, in the car park, in the street. She
couldn't cry or lie down in public. She had to get
home, to be alone; only then could she give way
to what she felt.

She was only a mile from her flat when she ran
into the back of a lorry and the world
disintegrated into chaos for her.

It was days before she knew anything about
what had happened to her; time had become a
seamless garment of pain and sleep. She woke
from one to the other only to retreat again. Her
parents were dead and she had been an only
child, so she had no relatives visiting her, but
somebody sent her flowers; enormous bouquets
which the nurses showed her excitedly.

'Get well soon, I need you here, love, Johnny,'
they read from the card. 'Johnny Fabian! His

secretary has rung up twice to find out how you are!'

Megan had gazed at them with blank indifference. In the place where she was, Johnny had no real meaning. Nothing but pain had any meaning, including herself, for a long time; the drugs the nurses gave her could take away the pain, but they took away all the significance of memory, too. It wasn't that she forgot, so much as that she did not think of anything outside those four pale walls and the threat of the pain.

When she did start the slow drift back to life, Johnny was her first visitor. She and her little room were prepared for his visit as if he was royalty; by then Megan was capable of sensing the air of excitement pervading the whole ward. Johnny Fabian was a national figure; his show was always close to the top of the TV ratings. The nurses chatted in low, elated voices while they waited for visiting hours to start. They seemed shocked that Megan was so calm about it all.

When Johnny did arrive, he brought more flowers. A basket of exotic fruit, too, and magazines, a couple of fat best-sellers, several get well cards from the programme team, scrawled with personal messages and signatures. The nurses were impressed; Megan knew he had most probably asked his secretary to go out and buy everything, but all the same she was touched by his thoughtfulness. Johnny had more than charm; he had a kind heart. When he kissed her cheek, he tried hard not to look shocked at the sight of her.

Megan knew why he was avoiding her eyes; she

had seen herself that morning, and for the first time discovered both how very ill she had been and how gaunt and haggard she looked.

'I can see you're on the mend,' he said in a bright voice. 'You're looking great, kid.'

She smiled wearily at him. 'Thanks, Johnny.' It was nice of him to lie.

She asked him how everyone else was and he told her in a lively way, trying to boost her mood with his own energy. He didn't mention Devlin Hurst and she didn't ask about him. She wasn't yet strong enough to think about Dev; instinct made her protect herself from the pain of it. For the moment she was just concentrating on getting through each long, long day.

'When they let you out of here,' said Johnny before he left, 'we're going to send you to a convalescent home in the Cotswolds. You'll love it; it was a big manor house set in a park before they turned it into a nursing home. It's got a gymnasium, jacuzzis, indoor swimming pool, saunas—you name it, they've got it, and if you get bored with that lot you can always just take a walk in this beautiful parkland. More like a good country hotel than a hospital, really.'

She tried to laugh. 'I shall be too exhausted to come back to work after a few days there!'

Johnny gave her an odd look. 'Your job will be open for you whenever you come back,' he quickly said.

After he had gone, she wondered about that—the strange glance and the hurried reassurance. How ill was she, and how long would it be before she was back to normal? Worry kept her awake, and when her specialist came to see her he noted the insomnia marked on her daily progress report and asked about it.

She frankly told him what was bothering her and he sat on the edge of her bed, lifting the tails of his spotless white coat first and apparently quite oblivious of Sister's flared nostrils. It was a ward rule that nobody—nobody at all—ever sat on the side of a bed, but Sister didn't utter a syllable. She just took a deep breath and tightened her lips.

The doctor took Megan's hand and patted it. 'I think you're up to hearing the facts now,' he began ominously, watching her pale face. 'I'm afraid you will not be going back to work for quite a while. You have some plastic surgery ahead of you when you're strong enough.'

Her free hand involuntarily flew to her face and the doctor half smiled, half sighed, shaking his head. 'No, not your face, your body. At the moment you have some scarring after the operation we had to perform when you were first brought in. A good plastic surgeon, however, should be able to disguise all that—you may even be able to wear a bikini again in time.'

He watched her face quivering, and frowned. 'You know, you're lucky to be alive, Miss Carr. You could easily have died from your very serious injuries. Our operating team worked like demons to save you—you have a lot to be thankful for.'

The ward sister stared at her, gimlet-eyed,

daring her not to be grateful.

'I am very grateful, Mr Oliver,' Megan said huskily, and he waved the words away with a peremptory hand.

'I did my job, now I want you to do yours—and fight your way back to normal. It won't be easy, I am not going to promise it will be—you'll get tired, dispirited, depressed, but if you make yourself hold on, in time you'll get there.'

She forced a smile, nodding. 'Thank you.' Sister's stare made it clear that the great man has spent more than enough time on her, and she should let him go.

He rose, smiling properly. 'Good girl. I'll see you again in a few days and then we'll discuss a date when you can move on to this expensive convalescent home! I know the place; only wish I could spend a few weeks there myself!'

Laughing, he walked on, with his attendant entourage of students and nurses, escorted by Sister every inch of the way.

It wasn't until his next visit that Megan discovered the full consequences of her accident and the following operation. The specialist hadn't allowed her to be told until then because he wanted to be certain she was mentally strong enough to stand the shock of the news.

He told her himself, quite gently. Megan stared blankly at him as it sank in, and he frowned.

'You understand?'

She was white, her skin ice-cold. She slowly moved her lips and heard her voice saying casually, 'Yes; I will never be able to have a baby.'

He looked disturbed, and picked up her wrist. 'Sister!' he snapped and Megan heard the flurry of movement, the prick of a needle. She felt annoyed because she had been very calm about it, hadn't she? She hadn't screamed or begun to cry. But they hadn't given her a chance to protest; she already began to feel light-headed. She closed her eyes and sank into the strange, muffling sleep she now recognised: drug-induced and disorientating, it was nothing like real sleep, and she never woke from it feeling fresh and restored. This time she did not even want to wake from it at all.

A week later, she was driven in a small, private ambulance, out of London to the Cotswolds convalescent home. By then, she was allowed up for most of the day, although she still had to rest a good deal. Physically, she was healing. Her state of mind was something else again; she was silent and withdrawn and often sat by a window, staring out across the parkland, her face blank.

'You aren't mixing with the other patients— why?' asked one of the nurses, a large girl with a horribly cheerful manner.

Megan frowned. 'I prefer to be alone. When can I go home? I'm fit enough now.'

'There's a good film on tonight, everyone will be watching it in the video room—why don't you come down?'

'No, thanks. I want to finish the book I'm reading.'

The place was run like a hotel; the nurses were only there in case of emergency, but they still kept a watchful eye on everyone and Megan was always glad to get away from that sensation of being watched. She had her own room with a lovely view of the lake and of woodland beyond the edge of the park, and she liked to stay there, rather than mix with the other patients. Only when pressed did she use the facilities available: the indoor pool, the saunas, the gym. She was perfectly well, she kept telling Johnny. 'Once I'm back at work I'll be fine! That's what I need—normal surroundings!'

The truth was, though, that she had no energy or spirit. Something inside her had broken with the news that she could never now have a child.

She had spent days brooding over what to do about Dev. No letter had come from him yet, but then he had warned her that it might be weeks before she heard, because he would be very busy before setting off on this great journey along the Amazon and might only have time to scribble her a note at the last moment.

He had been angry with her when he flew from Heathrow, and she didn't really have a clue how Dev felt about her any more, but one thing was crystal-clear to her—she had to end their engagement, anyway.

Dev was getting married because he wanted children; a home and family. She couldn't give him that now and so she couldn't marry him. If she told him the truth, Dev might feel obliged to lie out of pity or kindness. He might deny that he wanted children, or suggest they adopted, and, ironically, if she had not heard him talking to his sister she might have believed him, because she loved him enough not to care whether he could give her children or not. If the position were reversed, she would always have preferred to have Dev and no children than a chance of children with any other man, but how did Dev really feel about her?

She didn't know, and she couldn't tell Dev that she had overheard him and Emma talking. He must not know how much she guessed.

He had told her to write and let him know frankly if she changed her mind, if she found someone else while he was away, so that was what she did, at last, when she had nerved herself to do it. She wrote to Dev and told him she had met someone else, she was sorry, and ended the short letter, 'Goodbye, Megan.' Those were the two hardest words she had ever used; she agonised over them before she wrote them, and once the letter was in the post on its way to South America and Dev she spent a lot of time alone in her room, crying.

By the time she left the convalescent home she had used up all her tears and had learnt how to smile again; with the lips, at least, if not the eyes.

Her most frequent visitor throughout those weeks was Mark Bond. He had turned up one day, soon after she arrived in the Cotswolds, bringing an armful of flowers: roses and white iris and feathery gypsophila.

'I'd have come sooner, but Fabian told me you

weren't allowed visitors yet.' He dropped the flowers on her bed and stood back to stare assessingly.

Megan knew she was pale and lifeless, but she was too weary to smile. '*La Belle Dame Sans Merci*,' Mark murmured, and, incredulously, she laughed—the first time she has laughed spontaneously since her accident.

'What?'

' "Her hair was long, her foot was light, and her eyes were wild",' he quoted, a glimmer of teasing in his eyes.

'You're crazy,' Megan said, a faint pink rising in her cheeks as she remembered the rest of the poem.

Mark was remembering it, too. ' "I shut her wild, wild eyes with kisses four",' he quoted, sitting down next to the bed.

'Sister wouldn't approve,' she assured him, shifting on her pillows.

'She doesn't like Keats?' he blandly enquired.

'I doubt if she knows anything about him or his *Belle Dame Sans Merci*, but if she did, she wouldn't approve. There's a lot Sister doesn't approve of!'

He roared with laughter, which brought a capped head around the door, 'Not too much noise, please,' Sister said stiffly. 'Some patients are resting at this time of day.'

'Sorry,' Mark got out in a choked voice, and she nodded and vanished again. When she had gone Mark began laughing again, less noisily, and Megan couldn't help laughing, too.

Later, when she was alone, she realised that his visit had lifted her. She was glad he had come, and as the weeks passed looked forward more and more to his arrivals. By the time she was back home and able to start work again, Mark had become part of her life. They weren't lovers, they were friends, and the warmth between them made the loss of Dev more bearable.

Autumn had passed into grey winter long ago; she has missed all the rich warm colours of the falling leaves and the transitory sunshine. Megan came back to a cold city; to a quiet Christmas and a New Year which she found far from joyous. She has never been a creature of sharp mood-swings; in the past she has usually been even-tempered and contented, but that was before fate struck and deprived her both of the man she loved and any hope of ever having children or a normal marriage.

Before leaving the convalescent home she had had to go through several interviews with a psychiatrist. Meagan hadn't wanted to see her. 'I'm not sick,' she had said obstinately, refusing to keep the first appointment, but she had been persuaded to agree. The woman was middle-aged; thin and watchful with shrewd dark eyes. Megan had not liked the way she looked sideways, or the funny, superior little smile she wore when she did not like the answers Megan gave her.

'You ought to talk about your feelings; express them more openly. If you lock it all up inside yourself, you may have problems later. It's quite natural to feel bitter and angry. Anyone would, in your place; there's no shame in that.'

Megan had nodded without saying anything, and had been given that little smile again.

'You do feel bitter, don't you?' coaxed the other woman.

'No,' Megan said, smiling sweetly. Of course she felt bitter; she was angrily resentful of the trick life had played on her. She dreamt sometimes that it had not happened, and woke up in the darkness of night, face wet, listening to the indifferent breathing all around her. Life went on, whatever happened, but she felt her life had ended. She did not know how to cope with what had happened. She felt empty, desolate. She felt she wasn't a woman any more; she felt betrayed. But she wasn't going to talk about it to this woman. Why should she? She would never tell this woman how she felt. She did not like her. She wouldn't tell her the time of day. She hated the gleam of curiosity; the brightness of the eyes. Show me your pain, the other woman said; let me see it. But Megan wasn't telling her anything, and after she left the convalescent home she did not keep the further appointments that had been made for her. She ignored letters and phone calls, and in time the psychiatrist gave up.

Megan's own doctor saw her several times but did not get past the high stone wall she had erected to keep out all curious strangers. She might have talked about her feelings to someone close to her, but none of her friends were close enough, and she had no family. She had never realised until then how alone she was, or how much she had secretly wanted to build a family life for herself one day.

The pain of her situation was so intense that she could only cope with it, and Mark helped her there, without being aware of it, by being light-hearted, always fun to be with, which allowed Megan to forget what she wanted to forget and laugh as though she had no troubles in the world.

One day in his studio he gave her a ball of clay and told her to try her hand at making something while he worked.

'Making what?' she asked, taken aback, and he shrugged, grinning.

'Whatever you fancy.'

'But I don't know how.'

'It doesn't matter how; just play around with the clay until you get an idea. You'll find it soothing, like making mud pies when you were a little kid.'

She laughed, but he had hit the nail on the head. It *was* soothing, she found. Her hands instinctively felt the clay; squeezed it in her palms, smoothed it with her fingertips, rolled it round and round, drew it out, gave it shape and new dimension, screwed it up again into a ball, and while she played with the plastic stuff she was absorbed and calmed, and smiled at Mark when he winked across the studio at her.

'I like it.'

'I knew you would,' he said quietly, and Megan wondered how clever Mark really was and how much he understood of what she had been going through.

As the days passed, his company meant more and more to her, although it still had no romantic or sexual hang-up. They were friends, nothing more.

She should have known that people would misunderstand the situation, but it didn't occur to her until she went back to work and rapidly realised what everyone was thinking.

It was Johnny who came out with it bluntly. 'Is it serious?' he asked and when she stared, at a complete loss, added wryly, 'You and Mark, I mean, don't pretend you didn't know that!'

'Mark's a buddy of mine, that's all!' Megan snapped, and Johnny laughed.

'Oh, yeah? Platonic, you mean? I don't believe in platonic friendships between a man and a woman. Between the sexes there's only one sort of relationship.'

Megan narrowed her eyes at him, smiling angrily. 'So what is there between you and me, Johnny?'

'I'm just waiting for my cue,' he claimed, grinning unashamedly. 'Is this it, Megan? Are you giving me a green light?' He put both hands around her waist, pulling her towards him, and bent to kiss her, but as his lips touched her mouth she pushed him violently away.

Johnny looked down at her, amused by her angry reaction. 'How about dinner after the show tonight?'

'No thanks,' she said through her teeth before walking off. She was having dinner with Mark, as it happened, and wished now that she hadn't arranged for him to pick her up at the studios, because someone from the programme was bound to see them and that would only add fuel to the gossip.

She tried to hurry off once they were off the air, before any of the team left, but Johnny chose that evening to get difficult because in researching one of that batch of guests she had somehow missed a vital piece of information.

'How could you let me make a fool of myself like that? It should have been in your notes! What do you think I pay you for?'

Johnny was nasty because he had tripped up in public, and Megan couldn't blame him for getting angry. She han't done her job properly; she didn't even know how she had come to miss something so obvious.

'I'm terribly sorry, Johnny, it won't happen again!' she stammered apologetically, and Johnny stared at her, mouth hard, then shrugged.

'I hope it won't! Maybe you aren't quite back to normal after your illness. I'll forget it this time, but for the lord's sake keep your wits about you in the future!'

He walked with her out of the building a few minutes later, his brows rising as he saw Mark in his car waiting for her.

'Now I see why you wouldn't have dinner with me!'

She was flushed and didn't answer.

'Which reminds me, did you know Devlin Hurst is coming back soon?' Johnny asked after a thoughtful pause, and Megan looked at him in shock.

'But he isn't due back for months!'

'He picked up a bug out there and has been ordered home! The rest of the team are going on and if Dev recovers in time he may go back and join them, but I gather they've already shot an enormous amount of film and he may stay here to start the editing and write the narration.'

Megan fought to look calm, but knew Johnny was watching her with a mixture of curiosity and half-malicious enjoyment. He wasn't privy to all the secrets of her relationship with Dev, but he had known that she and Dev were seriously involved before Dev left, and he knew that she had been seeing a lot of Mark Bond over the past few months.

'I'm sure you're longing to see him again,' he said, eyes teasing, and Megan managed a stiff little smile.

'Yes, of course. Well, goodnight, Johnny.' She walked away to get into Mark's car, feeling sick. Dev was coming home too soon; she wasn't feeling brave enough to face him yet.

CHAPTER FOUR

FOR days she was on tenterhooks, expecting any moment to see Dev walking into her flat, into the office or the studio—but time passed and there was no word or sign of him. She decided Johnny had been teasing, or else had heard some groundless gossip. Or perhaps Dev had fought off whatever bug he had picked up, and was not coming home until the full year was up? The relief was almost as unbearable as the tension of wondering when she would see him, and in a mood of euphoria she went to a party with Mark one evening, feeling better than she had for a very long time.

The party was being given to launch a highly publicised new drama series; the director had invited some big stars as well as lots of media people. There was live music, expensive food and good wine, and a threat of several of the stars singing for their supper.

'It should be fun,' Megan had told Mark, tongue in cheek, after telling him the names of the big stars.

'I was once asked to sculpt the lady,' he confided thoughtfully. 'In the nude.'

'Did you do it?' She glanced up at him as they danced, and he gave her a wicked grin.

'What do you think?'

'Did she commission it herself?' Megan could see the beautiful actress in a corner of the room, surrounded by men. She was still ravishing, even at forty-five. How did she look naked, though?

'A lover,' Mark said. 'They split up not long afterwards. I've no idea which of them kept the statue.'

Something in his voice made her look sharply at him. 'Did they fall out over you?'

Mark's brows lifted. 'You're uncanny, do you know that?'

'It wasn't hard to guess! You looked much too smug,' she mocked gently, and he tightened his grip on her slender waist, putting his cheek against her long, richly curling hair.

Megan was still smiling as her blue eyes gazed vaguely over his shoulder at the shadowy, crowded room. A haze of cigar smoke hung in the air, people either danced casually, shuffling close together, or they stood about drinking and talking above the little band playing a medley of popular songs.

'Hey,' said Johnny, looming up in front of her, and she said, 'Hi, Johnny!' smiling, before she saw who he had with him.

'Look who just arrived!' Johnny said, watching her face.

Her skin was icy, her eyes stricken.

'Hello, Megan,' Dev said, and managed to make the greeting sound like an insult. She hadn't expected him to be so angry; it bewildered her.

'Good heavens, Hurst, I thought you were up the Amazon for a year,' Mark said cheerfully, his arm still round her waist although they had stopped dancing.

'I had to come home for medical treatment,' Dev told him curtly.

'That sounds serious.' Mark had stopped smiling, a faint bewilderment in his eyes at the other man's brusque tone.

'It could have been if I hadn't had a course of drugs as soon as possible, but they say they caught it in time and I'm almost back to normal now. I'll probably be allowed to go back to South America next month.'

Johnny frowned. 'Is that wise, Dev? Isn't there a risk of re-infection?'

'A slight one, but I want to finish filming, even so.' Dev's voice was forbidding; he did not want to talk about it and resented Johnny's questioning, which was instinctive, of course. Johnny always asked questions; that was his method of interviewing, particularly when he met up with someone who did not want to answer questions at all. He had the bulldog mentality and it was his great gift as an interviewer. Megan was staring at the floor, but through her lashes she managed to absorb how Dev looked: his face had a new grimness, he had lost a lot of weight, his cheekbones showed starkly through his sunburnt skin and his clothes looked a little too big for him. Her heart turned over. Dev had been very ill and it showed.

'You shouldn't take the chance, should he, Megan?' Johnny said with that typical trace of malice underlying the words. He was having some peculiar fun at her expense, but she wouldn't let him see that she knew as much. She didn't answer, pretending she hadn't heard.

Johnny merely repeated the question. 'Should he, Megan?'

'I can understand it,' Mark calmly answered for her. 'Work comes first, doesn't it, Hurst? Even where our health is concerned!'

Dev's mouth twisted; he shrugged. 'Exactly.'

Megan dared to look up at him while he was looking at Mark, but a second later his grey eyes flashed sideways and she found herself looking into them. It was like looking at a frozen wasteland and she flinched.

Why was he so angry? He hadn't been in love with her; he had more or less admitted as much to his sister. Over and over again he had insisted that Megan should write and tell if she found anyone else; he had seemed quite calm at the prospect, almost seemed to expect it. She had been dreading his return because of the pain of seeing him again, but she had not been expecting Dev to look at her with such bitterness and contempt.

Several other people came over to join their circle at that moment, and the talk became very lively. Megan whispered to Mark that she was just going to powder her nose, and without even looking in Dev's direction hurried away.

The party was being held in a big suite in a London hotel. Megan walked through the crowded, busy foyer and out into the street. Across a traffic-jammed road lay one of London's royal parks; an oasis of smooth green turf and trees. She darted through the traffic, slowing as she reached the safety of the park. It was twilight; a chilly, raw day in February. There were very few people around and those she saw were bent, huddled in their winter coats against the biting wind. The trees were bare, their branches a confused black criss-cross against the pale sky.

Megan walked slowly, hardly aware of having no coat, or of the wintry weather. How dared he look at her like that? She felt as if he had struck her; those cold eyes had been like a blow.

Restlessly, she turned in her tracks to walk back to the hotel, and her nerves jumped as she found herself facing Dev at the far end of the tree-lined walk. Had he followed her out here? Or was it sheer coincidence that he had come to the park, too? Pretending she had not seen him, she swung round and walked hurriedly along a path to the left, but when she reached a bend in the path there was Dev again, coming towards her.

She glanced from side to side, looking for an escape, a way of avoiding him, but she could only get away by turning and running in the opposite direction, and that would be so childish, it would be a confession of guilt she was not going to make. If Dev had loved her it would have been different, but she knew he hadn't, and his resentment made her burn with anger.

'There was no need to run away from me!' he said bitingly as they met. Her darkened eyes seemed to magnify him; he looked very tall, very forbidding. He wasn't anyone she knew any more. Had he ever been? How much had she ever known about Dev? She had thought she knew him, she had loved him, yet all the time she had been living in a delusion.

'I wasn't running away!' She put up her chin defiantly, her long hair blown around her face by the wind.

'That's what it looked like to me.' His voice was as wintry as the weather in the streets. 'When I arrived, you were dancing with Bond happily enough. You certainly looked as if you were enjoying the party, before I arrived. Then you fled. If it was guilty conscience, you needn't worry. I won't make any trouble.' Their eyes met and he smiled tightly; it wasn't much of a smile and it didn't make her feel any easier, especially when he added, 'Does he know about us, by the way?'

She looked down without answering, her fingers twisting and knotting together. She hadn't mentioned any names when she wrote to say she had met someone else, but the one fact she knew for certain about Dev was that he was clever. Seeing her with Mark, he had put two and two together at once. Of course, he wasn't to know she had lied about wanting another man.

'It is Bond, isn't it?' insisted Dev, and she hesitated, then nodded without looking up because if she met his eyes she might find it harder to lie, even in silence.

Dev laughed humourlessly. 'I wouldn't have thought he was your type!' A spasm of pain seemed to tighten every muscle in his face, and Megan watched him, her blue eyes wide and dark with feeling, wondering if he was still quite ill, in spite of his denials. In the thickening dusk he looked even more haggard, his face thinner. Had he come close to dying? The very thought made her heart dive sickeningly.

'I'm sorry, Dev,' she broke out in a shaking, husky voice, her face white. That seemed to make him angrier, the line of his mouth tightened.

'Just tell me one thing!' he said harshly. 'Was it going on behind my back before I even left? That night I went to your flat and found him there I had my suspicions. Were you already sleeping with him?'

'No!' She was incredulous—how could he believe that? Didn't he know her at all?

'It was an intimate little scene, though, wasn't it?' He smiled, but it wasn't a nice smile.

'Are you calling me a liar?'

'Let's say that men have divorced their wives for less!' he drawled, his mouth cynical.

'I do not sleep with Mark and I never did!' she snapped, red in the face. 'Not that it's any of your business. If I chose to it would only be my affair.'

'His, too, I'd have said?'

The cold mockery made her want to hit him, but she bit down on the furious words trying to burst out of her, and fought to stay cool and collected. 'Actually, Mark had taken me to a civic function that night, a very respectable affair, but while he was driving me home his car broke down and as we were close to my flat he just came in to phone for a taxi.'

'And while he was waiting, you slipped into something comfortable and he lounged about on your carpet by the fire in his shirt-sleeves? I see.'

His sarcasm made her teeth meet; through them she grated, 'It was pouring with rain, we got soaked to the skin running to my flat and the taxi couldn't come at once, so I made us some hot chocolate . . .'

'A cosy bedtime drink,' he drawled.

'You've got a very nasty mind!' Megan snarled back.

'Maybe I have, but I didn't imagine that letter of yours, did I? I can't say I was surprised to get it, of course! There isn't a woman on earth who could be trusted to stay faithful while her man was a thousand miles away.'

'That isn't fair!' she burst out, forgetting in the hurt of the moment why she had lied to him about meeting someone else.

'Not fair?' he repeated harshly. 'I hadn't even left the country before you were seeing another man! And you accuse me of not being fair!' He caught her face between his hands and forced her head back, staring into her startled eyes. 'Why the hell did you let me make a fool of myself by proposing? Why . . .' He bit the words back, his mouth snarling. 'Oh, what's the point? Women are all the same; they love to play little games and they can never bear to let any man go, even if they don't really want him.'

'Dev, you've got it all wrong,' she whispered, eyes wide and glazed with unshed tears. It was so long since he had touched her; he was making it hard for her to think straight.

'Have I? I doubt it.' But he was watching her fixedly, his eyes uncertain. 'Did you blame me for going away, was that it?' he asked suddenly.

'No!' The question threw her, perhaps because there was some truth in it. It hadn't occurred to her before, but now she wondered—had she been secretly angry with him because he was going away for so long? But she had known he was going when they first met, she thought, frowning. It would have been stupid to be resentful. She had merely wished he wasn't going. Flushed and trembling, she shook her head. 'No, of course not!' she insisted, and was foolish enough to try to explain how she had really felt. 'I didn't blame you, I'd known from the start that you were going—but, maybe . . . well . . . but . . .'

His lips curled back in a hard sneer. 'But? But what did I expect, you mean?'

She tired to struggle free of his grip and he wove his fingers into her hair to hold her. They were standing very close now, and her heart was shaking her whole body. She couldn't look away from that dark, dominating face, even though it scared her. 'Don't!' she whispered, trembling, and her fear seemed to push him right over the edge, feeding his rage as wind feeds fire.

He swooped down on her, mouth relentless, forcing her lips to part under a kiss that was full of fury. He wanted to hurt her. Megan's eyes burnt with tears behind her closed lids, she writhed in his arms, but he held her too close, and after a moment she grew very aware of the warmth of his body beneath his fine silk shirt. Only then, as she touched him, did it really get home to her how thin he was! Her heart winced as she discovered the new, terrifying austere contours of his chest and shoulders. All bone and muscle, so little flesh. He must have been desperately close to death to lose so much weight in such a short time.

She was so absorbed in discovering what his illness had done to him that she had forgotten to fight, her body limp in surrender, her mouth trembling with compassion and feeling as, with tightly shut eyes, her hands gently explored the changes in his body, unaware at first that her touch was turning his violence into a hot sensuality.

Dev might never have been in love with her, but she had always known he desired her. Whenever they made love there had been this heated abandonment, and although he had never said to her, 'I love you!' the way he touched her was more eloquent than words and she had innocently imagined that only love could make him so passionate.

She would never be that naïve again! She broke off the kiss, dragging her head back and to one side, and Dev let go of her, his hands dropping to his sides as he saw her put a hand to her bruised mouth.

His dark brows dragged together and his mouth twisted with a sort of self-disgust. 'Sorry,' he muttered with a mixture of regret and defiance. 'I lost my temper.' He watched her, his teeth tightly clenched, then reluctantly asked, 'Did I hurt you?'

Megan didn't answer; she was too busy looking at him and worrying about him. His face was darkly flushed, his eyes restless; he looked as if he had a high temperature. 'Are you OK, Dev? It's chilly out here!' She shivered herself as the wind blew through her silk dress.

'I'm fine,' he said, frowning down at her. 'But you're cold—and you aren't wearing a coat! It was stupid of you to come out in that thin dress in weather like this!' He took off his own jacket and put it round her shoulders, and Megan was horrified. She slid it off and tried to give it back.

'I'm fine, Dev! You need this, not me!' Didn't he know how ill he looked? Or was he refusing to admit it?

He firmly clamped the jacket around her, held it there with his arm. 'I'll decide what I need, thank you. You'll have my jacket until we're back in the hotel, so let's hurry!' He made her run, encircled with his arm, and Megan's heart beat a violent tattoo all the way. Once they were in the centrally heated foyer of the hotel Dev halted and looked down at her, an odd expression in his eyes. He still had an arm around her, a fact of which she was fiercely aware, just as she was very conscious of being far too close to him.

Since that kiss, his mood seemed different, gentler and less angry, but, far from making her feel happier, that disturbed her because Dev might have picked up her true feelings, and that was the last thing she wanted. He must not have any reason to suspect that she still loved him. He might try to talk her into going on with their marriage, and she couldn't do that to him.

'We can't really talk here, can we?' he said. 'Have dinner with me tomorrow night, Megan.'

He smiled suddenly, and she saw again, for the first time that evening, the private charm Dev showed to few people. 'I'm sorry for my bad temper. When your letter arrived I was already hatching the bug that stopped me in my tracks out there. I went a bit crazy for a while; hallucinating, seeing things that weren't there—I thought at one time I was seeing snakes! Fever plays weird tricks with the mind.'

She was horrified by the revelation of what he had been through. 'Oh, poor Dev!'

'Don't look so worried!' he said, a fingertip brushing away the frown above her distressed blue eyes. 'I survived, but I came close enough to dying to realise I wouldn't leave much behind me, if I did go! That was one thing that helped me fight my way back—the need to live and get some good work done. I suppose a crisis helps to concentrate your mind. I'm going to work like a dog to put this series together, for a start, but that wasn't the only thing bothering me! I kept wishing I had a wife and children waiting for me! I'd wasted years of my life and maybe I wasn't going to get another chance. If I'd died then, who would have missed me? Apart from a few relatives and friends there was only you—and then you wrote to say you had met someone else!'

She bit her lip, wincing. 'I'm s . . .'

'Don't say you're sorry again! Just say you'll have dinner with me tomorrow.'

He sounded relaxed and much too sure of himself; all the rage had gone, and she stared at him uncertainly. She was tempted to say yes, her body still burned with the fever of that kiss in the park—but she knew she couldn't go. She mustn't take the risk. If she saw him again he would soon guess she still loved him, and once he knew that, she would have to tell him the real reason why she had written those lies to him. But that would make it so hard for him; she did not want Dev to carry the burden of guilt over her.

He had only jut told her frankly how much he wanted to have children—and she couldn't give them to him! She loved him and she wanted him to be happy, but he would never really be happy with her if she could not give him the children he longed for. Sooner or later the day would come when he would regret marrying her, and she would know, even if he tried to hide it. She slowly shook her head, and Dev's face hardened again, but before he could say anything a man's voice spoke behind him, and Dev stiffened.

'Oh, there you are! I've been hunting high and low for you! Where on earth have you been, woman?'

Megan pulled a pretence of a smile into her face as she looked at Mark. 'Sorry, it was so hot in there that I wandered into the park.'

'Into the park?' Mark looked blankly at her. 'On a day like this? You haven't even got a coat!'

'Yes, silly of me—anyway, were you wanting to leave?'

'Is that OK with you?' Mark was frowning as he observed Dev's grim face.

'Fine, hang on while I go to the cloakroom to get my jacket.' Megan didn't meet Dev's stare; she just hurried away, leaving the two men contemplating each other in a hostile silence. She had never talked to Mark about Dev; she had no idea if he had ever known about their relationship. Nobody at the studios had known that she and Dev planned to marry, of course. She had kept her own counsel about that, because Dev had wanted it that way, although she would have loved to tell everyone. She had been dying to talk about Dev and the marvellous fact that she was going to be his wife. She had learnt to keep secrets, though. Her job meant that she had to be discreet, if not actually secretive, and it had stood her in good stead when she had a secret of her own to keep, so she had accepted Dev's decision and hadn't confided in anyone at the studio.

She collected her jacket; but lingered in the pink and gold powder room, which had a cool marble floor and Venetian mirrors along one wall. She had to repair the ravages to her appearance. She contemplated her reflection with something approaching shock. Her face seemed so unfamiliar, almost disturbing. Dev's rough fingers had wrecked her hair, his kisses had smudged her rose-pink lipstick and her skin was shiny with perspiration. She spent quite a time making herself look as good as she had earlier, when she got to the party.

Megan knew she wasn't pretty; her features were too irregular and she was small and skinny. When she took the trouble to dress and make-up with extra care, though, she knew she had a certain appeal to some men, especially when she smiled. She had learnt from her own experience that a smile was a bridge between people; if you met a smile you felt more confident, you didn't have to be afraid you were going to be ignored or snubbed. She had often been a wallflower at parties until she realised that other people were uncertain, too, and since then she had always tried to remember to smile a lot. It still didn't make her pretty, but she had a host of casual friends.

If she had not been so shy and quiet, she might have had far closer friends, but, although she remembered to smile when she met people, she found it far harder to talk to them easily, the way Mark or Johnny did. It was only because Mark did all the work that their friendship had grown rapidly. She made a face at herself in the mirror. Why couldn't she be more like Mark? Laid back, happy-go-lucky, always relaxed?

She did not hurry because she was nervous of confronting Dev again, but Mark was alone when she got back. 'Why do women always take so long to collect a jacket?' he teased.

'Sorry,' she said, fighting down an impulse to look around for Dev as they walked towards the main door of the hotel. Had he gone back to the party or had he left?

'How about a little late supper? I know a great place on the way back to your flat.'

She smiled absent-mindedly. 'No, thank you, Mark. I ate too much at the party.'

'It's early to say goodnight, though!' He sounded wistful, but Megan couldn't bear the idea of talking to anyone just now. She needed to be alone to think.

Reluctantly, Mark took her straight home. 'Coffee?' he pleaded on the doorstep.

'I'm sorry, Mark. Not tonight. I'm half asleep already.' Her mouth moved in a mimicry of a smile, but her eyes were far away and he could see it.

He shrugged and bent to kiss her. Megan turned swiftly so that the kiss landed on her cheek, not her mouth.

Mark straightened, eyes narrowed, staring at her, before suddenly asking, 'Was there ever anything between you and Devlin Hurst?'

Her blue eyes widened, her skin flushed. 'What?'

'Never mind, I just got my answer.' He was frowning, his jaw tense. 'From the way he acted, I guessed at something of the sort, but I couldn't believe you wouldn't have told me. You never mentioned him. Why not, Megan? We've been seeing a lot of each other for months—why didn't you tell me about Hurst? Or was it over before he left for the Amazon?'

Megan couldn't bear any more. She had to get away. Huskily, she said, 'I don't want to talk about it. Goodnight, Mark.' She closed the door on him before he had time to say any more, and heard his footsteps a moment later as he walked away.

Megan shut her eyes on sudden, scalding tears. She liked Mark very much. She had come to rely on him more than she had expected; he had helped her through a bad time since her accident and she did not want to say goodbye to him, but their friendship would never be the same after tonight. She suspected Mark knew that, too. He had strong intuition, almost feminine intuition. Perhaps all artists do, she thought. Seeing Dev had changed everything; it had come too unexpectedly, before she was ready to cope with it. She felt as if she had had a high wind blowing through her life. Everything had been overturned, flung into chaos. She was afraid to look to closely at what had happened, but she was even more afraid of what was to come.

At the programme conference next day, their producer, Fanny Gordon, said, 'I see Devlin Hurst is back. We could have him on the show again, Johnny, what do you think? Interesting to hear how his trip's going, get him to talk about this nasty bug he picked up.'

Megan stared down at her notepad, her face stiff and pale. Please don't agree, Johnny, she prayed, but Johnny seemed quite enthusiastic.

'He's a good talker, why not?'

'Right! Which of the girls wants to handle that?' Fanny looked at the trio of researchers sitting opposite her. Megan didn't look up. One of the others could get in touch with Dev and arrange a return visit to the show. The idea of doing it froze the marrow in her bones.

'Megan knows him, don't you, Megan?' Johnny said softly, feline enjoyment in his voice.

She gave him a furious, sideways look and he laughed out loud.

'Oh, well,' said Fanny, 'Megan had better do it.'

There was no point in arguing; it would only draw attention to her and make them all curious, which was no doubt what Johnny wanted. He loved to amuse himself by teasing people and infuriating them.

Fanny was quite different; if she had had any notion why Johnny was suggesting Megan she would never have gone along with the idea. She was not the malicious type, but was sensitive and clever. It was her mind that gave the show its strength. Johnny was the up-front image; he performed what Fanny planned behind the scenes. They made a brilliant team.

As the meeting broke up, Johnny followed Megan out, saying happily, 'Don't forget to ring Hurst, will you, darling?'

'If you were a woman, I'd call you a bitch!' she muttered, and he laughed, apparently flattered.

Back in her office she contemplated the phone with dread. Would Dev be in his London flat, or at his family home in the country? With any luck she wouldn't find him at either and could just leave a message for him to ring Fanny. It was hardly necessary to do any research on him as he was a return guest; they had his history on file.

She grabbed up the phone and dialled the London number. 'Yes?' Dev's voice was impatient and she took a deep breath on hearing it. 'Hello? Who is this?' he demanded when she couldn't get a syllable out.

Megan pulled herself together. 'Hello, I'm speaking for Johnny Fabian . . .' She used her 'public' voice; calm and assured. It was just as well

Dev couldn't see her face.

It was his turn to be silent, then he said, 'Megan?'

'Yes,' she said brightly. 'Johnny asked me to get in touch and invite you back on the show for tomorrow night. We're sure the viewers will want to hear how your journey is going, and about your illness, of course, and why you've had to come home, and so on——' She was babbling, but she couldn't stop it, because she was afraid of what Dev might say.

'Come over,' he interrupted suddenly, and her voice broke off.

'Sorry?'

'Can you come now?'

She was shaking, but he couldn't see that. He would be able to hear the huskiness of her voice, though, so she tried to sound level and unflustered, without much success.

'Oh, there's no need for us to research you this time, I'm just ringing to ask if you can appear tomorrow night.'

'If you come over here now. Otherwise, forget it.'

'That's . . .' she began, then bit her lower lip.

'Blackmail?' He laughed ominously. 'Maybe, but if you don't arrive, tell Fabian to find another last-minute guest!'

The phone went dead and she looked at it with blank disbelief before slowly replacing it. What was she to do now?

CHAPTER FIVE

MEGAN stopped off at Johnny's office on her way
to the lift and found him dictating to his secretary.
Johnny was inundated with fan mail every day;
replying took up most of his mornings, and he
wasn't sorry to stop for a moment when Megan
walked into the room.

'Get hold of Dev, darling?' he mocked.

She gave him a cold stare. 'Yes, but he asked me
to go over to see him to discuss it, and I'm very
busy in the office with the clippings on the Italian
fashion model.'

Johnny grinned. 'Too bad, but Devlin Hurst is a
priority, and if he wants you to go and see him,
you'd better go.'

She considered him with irritation. He was
wearing his usual expensive tailoring; silk shirt,
silk tie, handmade shoes; all chosen to give the
utmost effect to his looks, that auburn hair, those
fluid dark eyes. You had to admit he looked
terrific. Johnny Fabian lived the good life and
loved it. His myriad fans had no idea what he
could be like behind that charming façade.

'Off you pop,' Johnny crooned, much amused
by her expression.

Without another word, Megan turned on her
heel. Behind her, Johnny called out, 'You look
simply gorgeous today, darling!'

She felt like slamming the door, but she wouldn't give him the pleasure of knowing he had put her into a roaring temper. Perhaps it was the necessity of being so nice in public that made Johnny often very tricky in private. He could be kind, or charming, or thoughtful, to his staff, when he chose—or he could tease, lose his temper, snarl at people. You never quite knew what to make of him, but one thing was certain. You couldn't afford to make an enemy of him, or you had to leave the team. Megan couldn't remember any of the girls quarrelling with him, but several men had come and gone because they simply could not stand Johnny.

Fanny handled him perfectly; she behaved like a duchess confronting a tiresome child, and Johnny always fell into line. Fanny was, perhaps, the only person in the world he was afraid of.

She had her car in the staff car park outside the studios, and decided to drive to Dev's flat, but got caught in a traffic jam en route. Megan felt an odd relief; she wasn't in any hurry to get to Dev. To occupy the time she switched on her car radio and listened to a music programme on the BBC while she renewed her make-up and ran a brush over her cloudy dark hair, to the amusement of the driver of the car next to her.

'Hey, beautiful! What about a date?' he yelled.

She grinned at him, but didn't answer because just then the traffic began to move again.

She started to feel nervous again as she walked towards Dev's front door. Butterflies fluttered in her stomach and her mouth was dry.

He opened the door almost at once and her heart thudded in her chest, seeming almost to shake her whole body.

'Hello, Megan,' he said in that deep, familiar voice and she murmured something, feeling light-headed. He was in casual clothes: dark trousers, a white ribbed sweater over a dark blue silk shirt. His dark hair was ruffled, his grey eyes brilliant.

'Come in,' he said, standing back. 'I have some coffee freshly made—or would you like something stronger?'

'Do you think I'll need something stronger?' She pretended that was a joke, laughing huskily. 'But no, thanks, I won't have either coffee or anything else.' Dev gave her a sideways glance, gesturing for her to go ahead into his beautifully furnished sitting-room. His home in the country had been furnished by generations of his family, it didn't really reflect his individual taste, but his flat did; he had chosen the furniture and décor, and it told you quite a bit about him. Cool, masculine colours for carpets and the blinds on the windows; golden Scandinavian pine for chairs and tables, highly expensive music desk with the very latest equipment—ultra-modern angled lamps, black ash bookcases crammed with a bewildering variety of books on very different subjects—the place was very classy, and had that lived-in look of a real home.

'Sit down,' he said behind her as she hovered near the door.

'I can't be out of the office for long,' she said, hesitating between the two deeply upholstered leather armchairs.

'Stand if you prefer it,' Dev said, his hard mouth crooked with mockery. She had never noticed before how large his pupils were; they gleamed like black jet as he looked her up and down—from her heavy head of hair down over her slender figure in a demure, pleated cream wool dress. It clung to her breasts and waist and flared out over her slight hips, swirling around her legs as she walked. His stare made her so edgy that she hurriedly walked towards one of the armchairs, but Dev moved too, getting between her and the chair, so that she found herself sitting on the cream leather couch, with no real notion how she had come to be there.

'Pretty dress,' Dev said, sitting down next to her.

'Thank you.' Her voice was rusty; she prayed he hadn't noticed. Producing her notepad from her handbag, she sat up straight, trying to look efficient. 'Shall we start?'

Dev leaned back, an arm wandering along the back of the couch behind her while he eyed her mockingly. 'Start what?'

Her face burned, but she wouldn't let him disturb her. 'Talking about what you're going to say on the show,' she said stiffly. 'Johnny would like some idea beforehand; just the general areas for questions, no need to use any sort of script. But you remember that from the first show.'

'I remember a lot of things,' he murmured, shifting closer on the couch so that his thigh touched hers. At the same moment she felt his fingers brush along the nape of her neck. A shiver ran down her spine and she started up, wild-eyed and alarmed.

'I didn't come here for that!'

He caught her waist and pulled her down again, laughing. 'What did you come here for?'

'You blackmailed me into it!'

'So I did,' he coolly admitted, leaning over her, a little smile twisting his lips.

'Dev, let me go now, please,' Megan begged unsteadily, trying not to look at his mouth because she knew that that would be a bad mistake. She had dreamt about kissing him far too often; that mouth could tempt her into folly.

'You only just got here!' He had a hand planted on either side of her head; he had pushed his fingers into the wild flurry of her long hair against the back of the couch, and she wouldn't be able to escape without getting hurt.

'Don't do that!' Eyes dilated, she stared up at him, her throat pulsing with a growing fever.

'You're in love with another man—why should you be so hyper-tense about being alone with me?' he asked softly, watching her mouth. She knew he was thinking of kissing her, and her lips began to quiver, full and hot already as though he had been kissing her for a long time.

She was too disturbed to answer. She had to look away because she couldn't bear the way he was looking at her.

'Or . . . are you?'

She frowned uneasily. 'Am I what?

'In love with someone else?'

Her lashes flew up again; her blue eyes looked into his and found them closer; far too close. His body was touching hers now; he was leaning right over her, his face inches away.

'You know, I . . . I told you!' she muttered, utterly confused.

'Oh, you told me,' he said very softly, the words murmured out against her mouth. 'I was hundreds of miles away then, but now I'm here, so tell me again, face to face this time.' Their faces fitted like pieces of a jigsaw puzzle, mouth to mouth, hair mingling, breath mingling, and for the first time in months she felt complete, but she must not give in.

'Dev, I can't,' she moaned, shuddering as the tip of his tongue traced the outline of her lips. His hands were wandering intimately, too; her breasts rounded and grew heavy, her body was fiercely sensitive to the feel of his skin on hers. She was aching with a passion more intense than any she had ever felt before, perhaps because she knew she must stop him, yet it was so long since Dev had held her in his arms, and she had thought it would never happen again, and frustration had almost driven her crazy. Saying no this time would be the hardest thing she had ever done.

'Of course you can,' he whispered, smiling. He was sure of her, she could see that. She might be saying no, but her body was saying something else, and Dev's instincts told him so. Megan despised herself for being so weak; she had to stop this before it went too far.

'You're forgetting something!' she protested,

but his mouth went on teasing and tormenting her; lightly brushing her lips, touching and lifting again. He was playing games with her, and his eyes mocked because he knew she was finding it harder and harder to resist him.

'I never forget anything,' he said, his hands sensual, boldly caressing the warm curve of her body.

She was desperate to distract him, to put a stop to this torment. Pushing him away, she stammered, 'You have! You've forgotten Mark!'

Dev went on smiling, eyeing her mockingly. 'What about him?'

'You know very well that I . . . that Mark and I . . .'

'Why are you stammering, Megan?' he asked with a barbed little smile. 'Feeling guilty about something?'

'Guilty?'

He raised his eyebrows. 'Surely you know the word? Shall I spell it for you?'

She had been hot; now she was icy cold. 'Stop it, Dev!'

He pretended to frown, to look thoughtful. 'Oh, are you trying to tell me that you have to be faithful to Mark? Is that it?'

Biting the inside of her lip and tense with nerves, she nodded, and that was when he dropped the mimicry of a smile, the pretence of amusement.

'Why be faithful to him when you weren't to me?' The whipcrack voice made her nerves leap in shock.

'Let go of me!' She tried to sit up, struggle free, but his body was too heavy for her, even though he had lost so much weight. He might be thin, but the muscle and bone beneath his brown skin made him a formidable adversary to wrestle with.

'You must be kidding, sweetheart!' he snarled at her. 'I'm far from finished with you yet!'

She was rigid, utterly shaken as she saw that beneath Dev's smiles and sensual teasing he had been hiding a bitter hostility all this time.

'Don't talk to me like that!' she muttered, but the faint defiance got her nowhere, except that she made him laugh, and the hoarse sound of that laughter made her blench.

'Or what?' he mocked. 'What will you do to me? You can't fight me. You're too small and weak. You're like a bird, trapped in a room, fluttering about trying to get out and just smashing itself uselessly on the walls.' He lifted a handful of her hair and then let it float out around her white face. 'Even your hair is like feathers; soft and downy. When my fever was at its worst, I used to think you were there, with me, your head on my pillow, and I used to turn my face into your hair and let it cover me, like a tent. It made me feel safer.'

His mood seemed to have swung again; to be gentle, almost dreamy. Megan said uncertainly, 'Dev, I'm so sorry you were ill.' She was worried about him; he was so volatile, given to sudden switchback moods, and he had never been like that before he went to South America. What had this bug done to him?

'Are you?' He laughed and she winced.

'Yes!' His smouldering eyes told her that he didn't believe her, and that hurt. She looked at her watch. 'I'm sorry, but I have a lunch appointment at one o'clock. I must go soon.'

His face changed once more. In a businesslike voice, he said, 'But we haven't gone over the topics Fabian wants to discuss tomorrow night!'

'Well, obviously . . .' she began, but he interrupted.

'Look, I don't know about you, but I could use that coffee now.' He got to his feet, and walked away while she bit her lip, fuming. Dev was being bloody-minded, but she couldn't do much about it. Johnny would give her hell if she didn't make these arrangements for the show. Getting up, she followed him out of the room, into the beautifully equipped modern kitchen which faced out into a communal garden planted with well laid out shrubs and trees. Megan remembered vividly how delightful it was in summer; today it looked sad and forlorn in the raw grey weather, matching her mood.

'I really do have to go, Dev,' she said, running a hand over her ruffled hair.

'Not yet.' He was moving calmly, making coffee; he looked so normal that she decided that he had come out of that strange, worrying mood, and so she gave him a placating smile.

'Sorry, but . . .' she began and he turned, lip curling back in a snarl of violence which made her nerves jangle.

'I said not yet!'

She started to shake again and caught hold of the back of a chair; suddenly afraid she might fall down if she didn't grab something.

'Stop talking to me like that!'

'Stop arguing, then!'

'I have a job to do!'

'Then do it,' he coolly said. 'You came here to work out what Fabian would like to talk about—so work it out!'

She sat down at the kitchen table and laid down her notepad, gripped her pen in her hand, trying to look calm and collected and very efficient.

'Right, then,' she said huskily. 'First of all, your illness, of course . . . the viewers will want to hear about that.'

'Black or white?'

She stared, face blank. 'What?'

'Coffee—black or white?

'Oh, black, please.' He ought to know that; or didn't he remember? She remembered how he liked his coffee; she remembered everything he had ever told her about himself—that he always had his egg boiled for three and a half minutes, that he loved any sort of Chinese food, had a passion for hot cheese but never late at night because then it gave him indigestion, that he had once smoked cigarettes quite heavily until a friend bet him he couldn't stop, and was now glad he had taken up the challenge. Those were the little details love fed on, she would never forget anything he had ever told her—but had Dev ever loved her?

He was placing the coffee-pot and cups on a tray. She wrote the date and his name on the top of the page in her notebook. It gave her something to do with her hands; it helped her to feel relaxed.

'Now . . .'

Her voice trailed off as he walked past, out of the kitchen, back to the sitting-room. Megan had no option but to follow him. Dev was playing games with her and she felt like going now while she could, but she had the feeling he would ring Johnny and Johnny would send her back here. For some reason she could not fathom it was amusing Johnny to watch her struggling in the meshes of the net in which she was trapped, and Dev had shrewdly realised that Johnny was for the moment his ally. Or were they conspiring together? She frowned. Surely not? Johnny wouldn't—would he? And if he was—why? What was Johnny up to?

Dev laid the tray down on the coffee-table and sat down on the couch again. 'Will you pour?'

She silently obeyed and then sat down on a chair with her pad open on her knee and the coffee in front of her on the low table. 'Can we get on to business, please?' She didn't give him a chance to change the subject, just began firing rapid questions at him about the Amazon trip, writing down notes on anything he said that might make a good lead-in. This time Dev answered; he wasn't evasive or difficult, and she soon had a string of possible questions for Johnny to ask him.

She finished her coffee, glanced at her watch and got up. 'Then we'll see you tomorrow night; I don't have to tell you the procedure. See you in the hospitality room a couple of hours before the show.'

'Can't make it then,' he coolly said.

She did a double-take. 'But, I thought you had

agreed to come on the show tomorrow!'

'Yes, but I can't get to the studio until later—half an hour before the show starts, OK?'

Megan bit her lower lip, frowning. 'It will be cutting it a bit fine. Johnny likes guests to arrive well beforehand so that he is sure everything will go as planned.' It was one of Johnny's nightmares that one of his star guests wouldn't turn up. They always had someone else on hand, but of course they couldn't ask a 'big name' to hang around in case he or she was needed, and so that meant a second-rate show if a top guest failed to arrive. Johnny hated that idea. He started panicking early, sent his secretary to all the dressing-rooms to check that the guests had arrived. If one of them was late, Johnny went into shock.

'I'll be there!' Dev shrugged, and Megan eyed him with uneasiness.

'I hope you will—I shall get into trouble if you aren't!'

He walked her to the door, smiling blandly. 'Don't worry!' he urged, but Megan couldn't help doing that. Dev was in a worrying mood. It wouldn't surprise her if he didn't turn up for the show. She had not liked the way he looked at her when she said that she would get into trouble if he didn't arrive on time, and he hadn't bothered to hide the glint of menace in his eyes. She was sure, in fact, that he had wanted her to see it. Dev was still angry with her.

'Have dinner with me tonight,' he said, looking down into her troubled blue eyes.

'I'm sorry, I have a date.' She started to walk

away, but he caught her elbow.

'Break it.'

'I can't do that!'

'You will, though.' He sounded amused again, but under the light tone ran a note of threat and Megan looked at him with apprehension. Was she imagining all this? Dev had never been the sort of man to blackmail and threaten a woman—or had he? She had always known he could be ruthless, she had known he had a very strong self-image. He was a high flyer; a man of energy and drive with a lot of ambition and a strong ego. She had hit that ego; she had attacked his idea of himself, and just at a time when he was weak. Illness was always a low point for anyone, and she had unknowingly delivered her blow to his ego while he was very ill. She knew from her own experience how vulnerable you could be when you were ill.

What had it done to him when he got her letter? she wondered, her eyes on his hard face, her face pale between the thick masses of her long, dark hair.

'Oh, Dev, please,' she whispered. 'There's no point . . . it's over between us—can't you just accept that and let it go?'

His face was frighteningly rigid, bones clenched, mouth a white line. 'No.' The word had a volcanic force and she began to shake.

'Dev . . .'

'No!' His voice overrode her low, thready whisper.

She stared at him and he bent towards her. 'I don't let go of anything I still want, Megan, and I don't accept that it's over. It won't be over until I say so.' He straightened again and said in a level tone, 'Dinner, tonight, Megan, or . . .'

'Or what?' she said when he paused. She tried to sound offhand, indifferent, but her voice wavered, and he smiled then; a hard twist of his mouth which was really no smile at all.

'I'll pick you up at seven. My regards to Fabian.' He let go of her and stepped back into his flat. The front door shut and Megan stared at it for a moment, realising the threat he held over her.

Either she had dinner with him tonight—or he wouldn't turn up tomorrow; Johnny would have a nasty big hole in the middle of his show. Of course, Fanny would have a stand-by guest on hand in case of a problem, but the show would not be as good, and Johnny was going to blame Megan.

She liked her job, she was ambitious and wanted to move on at the right time into production. She would do a spell on the studio floor, she had her name down for a course on camera work. She was eager to learn and prepared to work hard to get what she wanted, but being fired by Johnny Fabian because she hadn't done her job well enough wouldn't do her career chances much good.

She drove back to the studio, and walked into Johnny's office to find him cheerfully entertaining a reporter.

'Hi, come in, Megan!' he lilted, holding out an arm and clasping her to his side. 'This is one of my little elves, Mac; God knows what I'd do without them. Megan, this is Mac, say hello to the nice reporter.'

Megan said hello and forced a smile. The reporter was looking nervous; Johnny's remorseless good humour was getting to him. Men never liked Johnny much, especially when he was terribly jolly with them. His women fans loved his whimsy and his jokey moods, but men never quite knew how to take him.

'I'll come back later,' Megan said, trying to look elfin.

Johnny called after her, 'See Hurst, did you?'

'Would that be Devlin Hurst?' asked the reporter, eyes lighting up. 'Isn't he just back from this trip up the Amazon? He coming on the show, Johnny? When? Tomorrow?' He started scribbling a note and Johnny winked at Megan, well pleased with this immediate interest. It told him that his instincts had been quite correct—the public would be fascinated to see Devlin Hurst on his show again.

Megan was not so delighted. She went back to her own office and sat behind her desk in gloomy contemplation of the obvious. Having announced to the Press that Dev was to be on the show, Johnny would be furious if he didn't show up. Even if he didn't fire her, he would make life unbearable for days. Johnny could be very nasty if he felt you had let him down. She had to make sure Dev turned up, and that meant that she must have dinner with him.

As soon as she had taken the decision she felt as if a great weight had been lifted from her shoulders, leaving her light and almost euphoric. She picked up the clippings file on her desk and began to do some in-depth research on the background of an Italian model whose love affairs had made her far more famous than her career had ever done.

It wasn't until much later, when she was at home, in her flat that evening, that she faced the truth about how she felt, her mouth wry in angry self-mockery. Who did she think she was kidding? She wanted to see Dev again. She was only too ready to fall for his veiled blackmail. He had simply given her the excuse she needed. If Dev hadn't made the pace, she would probably have been aching to see him and might have thought up some reason for visiting him. The fact was, she still loved him desperately and she always would. There was nothing she could do about that, but with a sinking heart she admitted that she was giving in to a dangerous weakness, one that could destroy both of them.

She mustn't forget why she couldn't marry Dev. His bitter rage over the breaking of their engagement must not make her forget that she had done it for his sake, and that nothing had changed. She could not marry him, and tonight she had to make that very clear to him.

CHAPTER SIX

MEGAN rang Mark at his studio flat to explain that she had to break their date, but he was out. She had to leave an apologetic message on his answerfone. She said she had to work that evening, which was one way of looking at it, since she was having dinner with Dev to make quite sure he turned up for the Fabian show tomorrow.

At the same time, it was half a lie, because her date with Dev was really entirely personal, and Mark would be very suspicious if he found out who she was seeing instead of him, so she made her message very vague. He had already showed signs of jealousy, without knowing anything about her past relationship with Dev.

He had no right to be jealous, of course. They had never been anything more than friends. Maybe they might have done, if things had been different, but Megan hadn't wanted to have a new romance.

She took ages to get dressed because she kept changing her mind about what to wear. She didn't want to wear anything ultra sexy or provocative because she didn't want to give Dev any ideas, but on the other hand all her female instincts made her want to look her best. In the end she chose a smoky blue taffeta dress cut on simple lines with a scooped neckline, tight waist, full rustling skirt ending at the calf, and the most gorgeous balloon sleeves finishing with a tight-fitting cuff buttoned with mother-of-pearl discs which shone in moony splendour every time she moved her hands.

She had bought it recently for a first night to which Mark had taken her, so Dev had never seen it. She brushed her hair upwards from the temples and fastened it in two wings with art nouveau combs decorated with mother-of-pearl and a silver Celtic maze design. Those she had found herself among a box of assorted junk at a country auction in the Cotswolds. She had bid on impulse and most of the contents of the box had been quite ugly and worthless, but finding the two combs had been a great thrill. They had been dirty and lacklustre; at first she hadn't realised their beauty, but when they were cleaned their real value emerged. They had become her favourite possessions; she loved the way they shimmered when she turned her head. In soft candlelight they were quite magical, especially when she was wearing the smoky blue dress, which matched them so well.

Just as she was putting the finishing touches to her make-up, the doorbell rang. Surprised, she glanced at her watch. Dev was early! She took a final look in the mirror and was pleased with what she saw, which in itself was dangerous. Her skin glowed with warm colour, her blue eyes were too big and too bright. She looked far too excited.

Turning away quickly, she walked to the door, snatching up her short silvery fur jacket on the way so that Dev should have no excuse for coming into the flat. She did not want a repeat performance of what had happened at his flat earlier that day. She was going to keep things low-key this evening.

Pulling open the door with a cool smile on her lips, she did a double-take. 'Mark?'

He laughed. 'Who were you expecting?'

Megan was pink with embarrassment, stammering. 'I'm sorry, Mark, I'm afraid I can't come to the theatre with you tonight. I have to work.'

His smile died as he stared at her. 'To work? What does that mean?'

'Johnny sprang it on me very late—I did try to let you know as soon as I could, but you were out. I left a message on your answerfone.'

'I haven't been back to my place,' Mark said with a frown.

'No, obviously, what a pity. I'm terribly sorry you've had a wasted journey over here, and . . . but you must go to the play yourself, I've heard it's wonderful.' She tried to joke about it. 'You'll be so enthralled you won't notice I'm not there.'

Mark grimaced. 'That I doubt.' His eyes wandered over her and he whistled. 'You look sensational, too! Where are you going dressed up like that? A première again?' The last time she had had to break a date it had been to accompany Johnny, Fanny and a couple of others from the programme team to a film première in Leicester Square.

'No such luck,' she said, evasively looking at her watch. 'If you're going to get to the theatre before the curtain goes up, hadn't you better be on your way? Some time, you must let me take you to a play to make up for tonight.' She was getting very nervous because Dev might arrive at any minute and she did not want Mark to see him.

'Megan, why don't you just skip whatever Fabian had lined up for you?' Mark put a hand to her cheek, stroking it as he stared into her eyes, smiling at her. 'It seems a pity to waste the way you look on that idiot!' He leaned forward and kissed her softly, whispering, 'We could have a marvellous evening, the two of us.'

Megan put a hand on his shoulder to push him away, hearing footsteps coming up behind him. She looked past Mark, her eyes very wide and dark as they met Dev's. His face was hard, unsmiling; he had seen that kiss. His icy grey eyes flicked over her with contempt and she felt like bursting into tears for an instant, before she got angry. Who did he think he was? How dared he look at her like that?

Mark had realised that they weren't alone any more. He turned round, stared and at once began to frown, his face altering.

'Hurst!' he said, his voice thick with suspicion, and slowly looked back at Megan. 'I suppose *this* is your "work" for tonight. I have been slow on the uptake, haven't I? I should have remembered the way Fabian ordered you to chat me up to get me on his show. Your job description may be as a researcher, but there are other words for it!'

Her face burned at the tone, the implication, but before she could react Dev did it for her. 'Don't talk to her like that!' he snarled, and then he hit

Mark. Mark hadn't been expecting that; Dev took him off balance and Mark flew sideways, hitting the wall before sliding downwards.

Megan made high-pitched little moaning noises as she ran and knelt down beside him. 'Mark, are you hurt? Oh, your head's bleeding . . . does it hurt? Let me see . . .'

He gave her a furious look, his face dark red but a white line around his mouth. 'Let me alone, for God's sake! I'm fine.' He staggered to his feet, glaring at Dev. 'That was a lucky punch, mister. I wasn't on my guard, but I am now.'

'Please, don't fight!' Megan protested, trying to make them listen, trying to get between them. 'Mark! Dev!' Neither of them took any notice; Mark had just managed to return the punch Dev had given him and Dev reeled back for a second, only to rush at Mark again. 'Stop it at once! How dare you fight over me, as if I were a squaw?'

They weren't listening, and looking at their set, aggressive faces Megan wondered if she was really what they were fighting over anyway! For some reason they hadn't liked each other on first sight; they were both very masculine and brimming with the competitive spirit, and not only over her, either.

Megan was not going to be used as first prize in a boxing ring. She was sick of the whole situation; sick of both of them, too. She watched them circling each other outside her front door, and then she silently shut the door on them, went into her sitting-room and turned on the television as loudly as she dared with the neighbours in mind. Now she could neither see nor hear them and when doorbell began to ring again she simply ignored it. They could both just go away and she hoped she would never see either of them again.

She should have known it was unwise to under-estimate an obstinate man. Ten minutes later, while she was still sitting in front of a blaring tele-vision set, Dev walked into the room, and she leapt up incredulously.

'How did you get into my flat?'

'Broke in,' he admitted coolly.

'You can't do a thing like that!' she seethed, flushed to her hairline. 'Breaking into someone's home . . . it's against the law, it's burglary.'

He gave her a mocking look. 'So it is. What are you going to do about it? Call the police?'

'I ought to,' she said angrily. 'How did you do it? If you've damaged my property . . .'

'I haven't. I used a professional technique.'

She stared, dumbfounded. 'Professional technique.'

'I was burgled myself once, years ago. I caught the guy in the act. I should have called the police, but he hadn't had a chance to take anything yet and I suppose I was soft-hearted enough to feel sorry for him, so I let him go, but first I asked him how he had got in, and he showed me. I had burglar alarms fitted next day and new locks, but I noticed your lock was the same as mine had been, so I used the method my burglar had shown me, and it worked like a dream. You really ought to have new locks fitted to that door; and several, not just one. A chain lock would be wise, too.'

'I don't believe I'm hearing this,' Megan burst out furiously. 'You break into my flat and then give me a lecture on security!'

'You need one. Take my advice, call in an expert. It's amazing you've never been burgled before.'

'Get out of here before I do call the police!' she snapped, but he stayed just where he was, watching her.

'Aren't you going to ask about your boyfriend's health?' he drawled.

'Both of you make me sick! Acting like a couple of stupid little boys!'

'I hit him because he insulted you!'

'Nobody asked you to!'

'You're very ungrateful,' he said, smiling wryly, then put a hand to his jaw, as though the movement of his mouth had hurt.

'I hope Mark hit you hard!' She wasn't going to be sympathetic, so he needn't grimace or look sorry for himself.

'Your boyfriend has pretty solid fists. I shan't be able to laugh much for a few days, and I think one of my teeth is loose—but you should see him! Although I doubt it he will want you to until the bruises heal.'

His air of smug self-congratulation was infuriating. 'Will you go away?' she yelled.

'Not until you come with me,' he simply said. 'I must go to your bathroom first and do something about this cut on my cheek, have a wash and tidy my hair.'

'You don't really imagine I'm still going out

with you?'

He strolled to the sitting-room door. 'You'd better.'

'Don't you try to threaten me . . .' she fumed, and he turned and gave her a crooked little smile.

'I'm not threatening you, Megan. I'm making a promise! By the way . . .' His voice lowered, almost to a whisper. 'You look lovely.'

He vanished before she had got her breath back, and she put both hands to her hot face, trembling. It was rare for Dev to say anything like that. She could hardly believe he really had said it, especially in that voice, but she mustn't be weak, she must not let him get to her. It would be dangerously easy to let him coax her into changing her mind; all her own feelings were fighting on his side but her common sense and her honesty kept reminding her that it would be fatal, for Dev's sake. She couldn't tell him why she had changed her mind so she had to stick to her decision, whatever Dev said or did.

She was still arguing with herself when he returned, his dark hair brushed and smooth, the blood washed off his cheek, although there was still an angry mark there, and his beautifully cut suit looking a good deal more elegant than it had after the fight with Mark.

'Ready?' he enquired with that maddening assurance that she would do as he wished.

'I will come to dinner tonight,' Megan said carefully.

He smiled and her teeth met.

'But there are conditions,' she added.

He lifted one brow. 'Oh, yes?'

'You keep your hands to yourself all evening!'

He gave her an insolent look, but still said nothing.

'And this is the last time!'

'Oh, I don't think so,' Dev said, putting out his hand. 'Come along, I'm starving.'

She was still sitting there, her hands in her lap, and refused to move. 'Take me seriously, Dev!'

'Now?' he asked, and she felt her face burn.

'You know very well what I meant!'

He bent and his fingers fastened around her wrist, yanking her ruthlessly to her feet even though she fought against his strength. She was held close to him for a moment; he looked down into her eyes, the darkness in his frightening her.

'Don't provoke me, Megan, which means don't hand out ultimatums when you don't have the firepower to back them up. You and I haven't had our serious discussion yet, but it's long overdue. We'll get dinner out of the way and then we'll talk.'

'There's nothing to talk about, Dev!' She was afraid of talking to him; he might guess something, start putting two and two together.

He put a hand over her mouth. 'You know there is; we have to talk and the sooner the better. Now, come on! They may not hold our table if we're much later. This is a very popular restaurant; I was lucky to get a table at such short notice. I think somebody cancelled.'

The restaurant was small but exclusive and they had a table in a shadowy corner, where they were unlikely to be observed. For such a tiny place, the menu was enormous, and if Megan had had any appetite at all she would have studied the list with greedy enjoyment, but love made her indifferent to food and she just toyed with a game consommé followed by turbot, a fish she liked very much, which the restaurant served with an array of fresh green vegetables. Dev was less abstemious; he chose a rich terrine followed by duck in a wine and cherry sauce.

While they ate he talked about what he had experienced in South America: the terrible poverty he had seen, the charm of the children, the sadness of the old, the vast distances, mind-blowing colours and scents, the riotous confusion of the green forests. Megan listened, enthralled; he was a brilliant reporter even when he was talking off the cuff, his eyes gleaming with excitement, painting a word picture for her of the riot and confusion of the forests and the river's unpredictability. She could see it all—the sudden eddies and whirlpools, the glistening watersnakes, insects dancing always above the surface, birds calling high among the tall trees, hung about with creepers which dangled down into the river, the floating corpses of animals or birds which gave an oily smell to the water at noon, the morning and evening mists. The haunting images filled her imagination, and at last she understood why he had dreamt of going there. He had never talked to her like that before; she saw into his mind and bitterly regretted that this insight came too late.

'When are you returning to finish the filming?'

she asked over their coffee.

'In a couple of weeks, perhaps—I have to take some tests at a hospital, to make sure that my blood is free of the bug I picked up. They aren't sure yet whether or not it's a recurring fever, like malaria.'

She shuddered. 'How terrible! Should you risk going back?' She wanted to beg him not to return, she was afraid that next time he might die, but she had no right to protest; she could only hold her tongue and suffer.

'Unless my specialist tells me to the contrary, I shall go back and finish the job I started.' He smiled suddenly, self-mockery in his grey eyes. 'Anyway, I loved the place and can't wait to get back, for all the discomforts and dangers.'

She sighed. 'Yes, I understand that.'

'Do you?' He leaned over the table towards her, his brown hands resting on the white damask cloth. His fingertips reached out and touched hers and her own hands quivered. 'I had the idea that you wouldn't,' he admitted. 'You never seemed interested.'

'You never talked about it all the way you have tonight.'

He looked struck. 'Didn't I? No, I suppose I didn't. When we met I was straining to get over there; half of me was already there, in some ways. I'd lost all interest in everything else. Nothing but the Amazon seemed quite real to me.'

'Including me,' she murmured, and he looked sharply at her.

'That isn't true!'

'Isn't it? Sometimes when we were together I used to feel that I was just a shadow on a wall to you. You talked at me, danced, kissed me, but I never got through to the real man.' Her voice had a sadness he couldn't understand and she could never explain, because now it was too late and they were fated never to know each other.

His fingers moved again, twined with hers on the white cloth. 'I'm sorry, Megan. It was a crazy time in my life; a pity I met you while I was so obsessed with a dream—but even though it may not have looked like it, I had fallen in love with you.'

Megan's heart squeezed painfully, as if a giant hand had taken hold of it, and she looked down, fighting with tears. Did he mean it? Was it the truth? She couldn't remember him ever telling her he was in love with her; looking back over those meetings before he left for South America, she was sure he had often been evasive, as if afraid to say too much.

'I didn't have the time or energy to give you,' Dev was saying quietly, holding her hands. 'But I knew right away that you were the woman I wanted for my wife. I decided not to ask you to marry me until I got back from the Amazon. I didn't want to complicate matters while I had so much on my mind, for one thing, and for another I didn't think it was fair to you to ask you to give me any promises before I went away for such a long time. You're so much younger than me. I've been around and taken a few hard knocks—you haven't. I was afraid you would meet someone else and I didn't want you to have to feel guilty if you did.'

She kept her eyes lowered, a burning pain behind them. Dev had tried to protect her from the burden of guilt, and that was ironic now when she was trying to save him from the same bitter weight. He had told her why he wasn't asking her to marry him, but she could not be as frank. Honesty was not an option for her; if Dev knew why she had broken with him he might insist on going ahead with their marriage anyway.

He lifted her hands to his mouth and softly kissed her palms. 'But then you told me you loved me, and I knew I couldn't bear to go away without trying to hold on to you.'

She felt grief in her throat, like hot dust choking her. She pulled her hands free and blindly got to her feet.

'Excuse me, I must . . .' She couldn't get another word out and almost ran to the powder-room. It was fortunately empty; she could let the tears come, scalding and bitter, while she sat on a chair and rocked back and forth, her hands over her face.

When she stopped crying she washed her tear-stained face in cold water and renewed her make-up, combed her hair, made sure there were no telltale signs of her misery for Dev to see before she went back to join him. By then there were other women in the powder-room; one of them admired her perfume and Megan stayed for a few minutes to chat, glad of the chance to practise her smile and her small talk.

She walked out with the other woman, still chatting about perfume, and Dev observed her with a wry smile.

'I was beginning to wonder if you'd been taken ill, but I gather you met a friend in there!'

She laughed gaily. 'That's right.' She didn't bother to explain. Looking at her watch, she said with pretended amazement, 'Look at the time! I must go, I'm afraid. I have to be at work early tomorrow morning.'

Dev was frowning, but he paid the bill and they walked along the street to where he had parked his car. Before they drove off, he sat with his hands on the wheel, staring straight ahead.

'You didn't give me an answer.'

Her nerves leapt. 'Answer?'

'I just told you I love you, Megan!' His voice was deep, harsh.

She had hoped to avoid this scene. She didn't feel strong enough to cope with it. She was afraid she was going to cry.

'I'm sorry, Dev,' she whispered, not looking at him.

'Sorry?' He flung round, staring. There was violence in the air; she shrank back in her seat, head bent, her long, dark hair hiding her white face. 'Look at me!' he snarled, but she shook her head.

'Please, drive me home, Dev.'

'And that's it?' He sounded incredulous. 'After all I just said to you, you can only say . . . drive me home, Dev?'

Megan bit down on her lower lip until it bled;

the salt-sweetness of her blood seeped into her mouth, but she felt no pain because her misery over Dev had anaesthetised her.

'You don't love Mark Bond! I don't believe it!' Dev wasn't asking her, he was thinking aloud, and she was afraid of what he might come up with if he started thinking. She had to distract him somehow.

'That night you proposed . . . at your party,' she said in a high, thin voice. 'You told me that if I changed my mind I only had to write and say so, that you'd understand and I wasn't to feel guilty—yet ever since you got back you've been hounding me, accusing me. I'm tired of it. It's over, don't you understand? Now, will you please leave me alone?'

There was a stunned silence, as though he couldn't believe she had spoken to him like that, then he swung round in his seat and started the engine. The car shot away with an angry roar. Dev was staring at the road, his profile jagged with rage. She caught a glimpse of it out of the corner of her eye and winced at the sight.

He didn't say a word all the way to her flat, and when his car screamed to a halt outside he just sat there, his hands on the wheel, his face averted.

Megan swallowed, then huskily said, 'Goodbye.' She had meant to say goodnight in fact, but she must have been thinking goodbye and that was how it came out.

Dev stiffened, his hand tightening on the wheel. She didn't wait for him to react; she dived out of the car and ran.

She didn't sleep very well that night, and in the morning she looked at her reflection with loathing. She was pale and dark-eyed, and even careful application of her usual dark pink blusher could not give her skin any sort of glow.

She knew people at work would notice. In their business, looks were everything, even behind the camera. She would get comments: sympathy, questions, a few catty remarks. If she had been offered odds, she would have bet on Johnny's reaction, and she was right.

He did a double-take when she walked in, and raised his brows at her. 'Darling, what happened to you? Or should I say who?'

One of the other researchers giggled.

Megan kept her temper. 'I think I'm coming down with a cold,' she said. 'Thanks for the sympathy.'

'You poor love,' Johnny said, keeping his distance but blowing her a kiss. 'Don't come near me, though. I can't afford to catch it. I've got a show to do tonight. Which reminds me, where are your notes on Dev Hurst?'

'On your desk,' said Megan with tart emphasis. 'Right in front of you.'

He looked down at the folder. 'Nobody told me.' Megan didn't comment on that.

'Fanny has a copy, of course,' was all she said, as Johnny opened the folder in a desultory manner, but before he had even started to read the door of his office was thrown open and Fanny hurried in, pink and excited.

'Guess who I've just managed to get for

tonight's show?'

Everyone stared at her. Nobody answered and she laughed, her eyes alight with triumph as she told them the name of one of the biggest names in movie history.

'Scrap everything else,' Fanny added, waving both arms as though clearing the room for action. 'We won't have any other guests. We're going to make this special; we'll devote the whole half-hour to her. We'll run several clips from her best films, of course.' She looked at the other researcher. 'Lyn—you can get hold of them from the distributor, and put together a few notes; questions for Johnny to use as lead-ins to the clips. You know what we want. Megan, you can liaise with her people for us. Ring her at the Dorchester—she checked in late last night, she'll probably still be asleep, but her Press agent will be there, or her secretary. Talk to them if you can't talk to her, and you probably won't be able to, but no problem. She's too big a fish for that to matter, so long as we can be sure of getting her here. That could be a problem; she can be temperamental . . .'

'Oh, God,' groaned Johnny, turning green.

Fanny gave him an indulgent look. 'Don't have kittens, Johnny. I'm sure she'll turn up.'

He wasn't reassured. 'I've just remembered what I know about her,' he muttered, running a trembling hand over his auburn hair. 'She never shows up for anything—including her own films!'

'This time I think she will.' Fanny looked smug and Johnny eyed her with a gleam of curiousity.

'Why are you so sure?'

She put a finger to her lips. 'Never mind. Let's just say I have my reasons.'

'Very mysterious,' said Johnny, and Fanny laughed.

Megan had been sitting there in chill disbelief. Obviously, Dev would no longer be needed for the show—and who was going to tell him that he had been dropped? She cleared her throat and Johnny looked at her.

'If we aren't going to need Dev tonight, we ought to let him know as soon as possible,' she said huskily, and Johnny beamed at her.

'OK, you do that.'

Megan bit her inside lip, frowning, very pale. She could not talk to Dev again; she couldn't face it. She had said goodbye to him when she wrote that letter to South America and she had said goodbye to him again last night. She couldn't bear much more of it. She felt as though she was bleeding slowly to death; a coldness seeping through her whole body. She didn't know if she really was ill, but she certainly felt ill.

'No, no,' said Fanny, face thoughtful. 'We may still need him, if she doesn't turn up. No point in telling him that, of course. We'll just keep him as a second string to our bow; a little insurance policy.'

Megan's throat burnt with sickness. It was a ruthless world they lived in; she was coming to think she wanted nothing more to do with it or them. If they got Dev along to the studio and then didn't use him, he would be so angry! He hadn't really wanted to do this second programme; she suspected he had agreed only in order to use it to blackmail her.

Surprisingly, Johnny disagreed, however. 'I think we should tell Dev, Fan. Dev's in the business. He'd understand.'

The producer stared at him, lips pursed. 'He still has an ego.'

Johnny said softly, 'That's just it. He knows too much about how we operate; we couldn't fool him that it was a last-minute decision. He understands the way things work, and he's a very clever guy. Ambitious, too! He's going places. He could be an important man around here one fine day and we wouldn't want him to have a grudge against either of us, would we?'

Fanny pulled a face. 'Now what have you heard, I wonder, that I missed?'

Megan watched Johnny, frowning. She had begun to wonder why Johnny was so careful to please and placate Dev, and now she knew. Johnny thought that Dev was potentially a good friend and a bad enemy to make.

Johnny grinned. 'Never you mind.' He wasn't going to betray whatever secret he had been told; he was far too sharp. Was Dev in line for some really big promotion? wondered Megan, her heart sinking. That would mean that he would be based here in the studio block, perhaps, and she might have to run the risk of seeing Dev every day. What on earth was she going to do?

'OK,' Fanny capitulated. 'So we tell Hurst that he may be dumped, and if he refuses to turn up, what then?'

'We can get one of our tame lions,' said Johnny,

grinning. They had a list of well-known names always ready to step into the breach if they needed someone urgently at the last minute; there would be no problem getting one of them.

'Very well,' said Fanny. 'Megan, ring Dev Hurst now; tell him how things stand, see how he reacts. If he says we can take a running jump, you'd better ring someone else.'

Megan swallowed, throat sore. 'Maybe he would take it better from Johnny.'

Johnny gave her a shrewd look, but Fanny surprisingly nodded. 'Yes, he probably would. Good thinking, Megan. Johnny, it would come better from you—don't you think?'

Johnny was still watching Megan; he gave her a crooked little smile. 'If you say so.' He picked up his phone and dialled. Megan discreetly left the office, her face cold with perspiration. She went to the cloakroom and spent a few moments renewing her make-up. When she got back to her own office she found Johnny there, flipping over the pages of her desk diary. He looked up, an odd expression on his face.

'You don't seem to have anything important down in your diary for the next fortnight,' he said, and Megan stared at him blankly.

'I suppose not. Why?'

'I talked to Dev Hurst,' said Johnny, and she stiffened, suddenly fearing what was to come, although she really couldn't guess what Johnny was going to say, only that from the look in his eye he knew she wasn't going to be too happy about it.

'He wasn't very flattered to be used as a stand-by guest, but he agreed to do it, on one condition.' Johnny paused, quite deliberately, watching her intently.

'What was that?' Her voice sounded very dry, very shaky.

'He is putting together a short programme trailing the Amazon series to be shown next spring, and he's in a hurry to get it done before he goes back to South America, so he needs a good researcher and assistant for a couple of weeks.'

Megan's nerves jangled; she was trembling violently. She knew what Johnny was going to say now and she was appalled. She couldn't do it; the very idea froze the marrow in her bones. Why was Johnny looking so amused, as though this was all a game just for his entertainment? Couldn't he see how it was tearing her apart? And, even more urgently, how on earth was she going to get out of it?

'He asked me to let him have you just for two weeks,' Johnny said, chuckling. 'And of course I said yes. I'm sure you'll have a fascinating time, Megan, working for him; great experience for you. A whole new area for you; you'll learn a lot.'

Megan simply didn't know what to say—she dared not tell Johnny she wouldn't work with Dev, because if she did she would have to tell him why, and she didn't want to do that. She could give in her notice, of course; leave the show—but if she told Johnny she was leaving right away it would be obvious why, and that would make Johnny very curious. She was in a trap and she knew who had laid the trap for her. Dev.

She wished she could hate him; it would be easier for her, but she couldn't. She loved him, and she simply did not know what she was going to do now.

CHAPTER SEVEN

SHE found Dev in a viewing room in the basement. 'He started work this morning,' Johnny had said, telling her where to find him, but, when Megan tapped on the door and was told to come in, she found Dev idly leaning back in a chair, his feet on a desk and his hands linked behind his head while he whistled tunelessly. There was no film running and the lights were blazing.

She stood there watching him with a feeling close to hostility, and Dev stared back with the same look on his face.

'Well, come in and shut the door.'

She didn't close the door, she took a deep breath and said fiercely, 'Dev, I am not going to work for you!'

'Have you told Fabian that?' He smiled mockingly, knowing she hadn't.

'Can't you see how crazy this is?' she broke out, trembling. 'Why are you doing it? It would be so much simpler if . . .'

'Oh, but I've never liked my life simple,' he drawled, swinging slightly in the swivel chair, his long, lean body totally at ease and keeping her eyes riveted, because she might hate him when he wore that insolent smile, but she couldn't help feeling the same old tug of attraction. He drew her as the north draws the magnet; she swung helplessly towards him deep inside herself, and fought it by remembering the pain which still kept her awake at night.

'You may not, I do,' she said, and he shrugged his indifference to that.

'I'm sure you do—but you aren't being given the option. Fabian told you my deal? I could get someone from the temp office people, but the lord alone knows who they'd send. I haven't got time to train anyone and I don't want some resting actress who is only interested in getting in front of a camera. You know this work, you'll at least be useful. The sooner I get this programme put together, the sooner I'll be on my way back to the Amazon, and you'll be rid of me for another six months.'

'Make it for ever and we have a deal,' Megan muttered.

He laughed without humour. 'Who knows? With any luck you may get your wish. I'm not going on a Sunday school picnic.'

She flinched, even paler, and frowning. 'If it's that dangerous, why go back at all?'

'I thought you wanted to get rid of me!' he said softly, and she bit her lip.

'I . . .'

He moved with the lightning strike of the cobra; one moment still and poised, his eyes fixed on her, glittering, and the next getting out of his chair and reaching her in two long strides. She didn't have time to think; she felt his hands clamp down over her shoulders, pulling her up against him, and she gasped, recoiling from the contact with his body as if he was white-hot.

'You look shocked,' he murmured, smiling with satisfaction.

'Why are you doing this?' she protested, looking down because she couldn't meet those grey eyes or they might see what she was feeling. 'You're just making it harder for yourself. It is over, Dev, it's over, please, just let me go, stop this.'

He lifted one of those heavy hands and now it was light, sensitive, his fingertips gently caressing her throat, making the tiny downy hairs on her pale skin shiver and sway in answer to his warm flesh. Her body always betrayed her; she was her own worst enemy, and Dev knew just how to use her sensual weakness against her.

'I told you—it will be over between us when I say so and not before,' he said, his lips stirring the dark tendrils of her hair, making her moan almost inaudibly, her eyes closed.

'I hate you,' she said without any real hope of making him believe her, yet half meaning it, because he was ruthless in pursuit of what he wanted and she felt like a trapped little animal. She ought to fight him with weapons he understood—hit him, scream, turn violent—but she needed all her energy just to fight the terrible drag of her desire for him, and she wasn't, anyway, the type of woman who was forceful. She had never been a dynamic career-woman, although she wanted to be successful in her job and meant to climb the company ladder, if she could. She would have to do it her own way, though—she couldn't play a cut-throat game of politics or cheat or bully her way to the top, any more than she could ever

sleep her way upwards, although the
opportunities were always there in this business.

She forced her eyes open and made herself stand
stiffly, a cold little statue in the circle of his arms.

He was gently kissing her neck, one hand
moving down her spine, fondling her back.

'You're so delicate, do you know that? Lovely
and delicate; you remind me of Snow White—not
the schmaltzy film, she was just a pretty wax doll,
that girl. No, the girl in the story, the original
story; about the king and queen who couldn't
have a child, then the king shot a black bird and it
lay on the white snow, a drop of red blood on its
breast, and the queen had a child with hair as black
as night, skin as white as snow, and lips as red as
blood. The first time I saw you, that was what I
thought of . . . you had that doomed look.' He
laughed, but Megan wasn't laughing; she was
standing straight and rigid, her blue eyes wide and
sombre.

Dev drew back a little to stare down at her, and
his smile died. 'And you are,' he said with a touch
of cruelty. 'Doomed, I mean. You aren't getting
away from me, Megan, at least for another two
weeks.' He put a possessive hand around her
neck, as if he meant to strangle her. 'And you can't
get out of it because Fabian won't back you up if
you make trouble—try it and see.'

'What have you got on Johnny?' she asked
angrily, and he laughed.

'I haven't got anything "on" him, as you put it.
I'm not leaning on Fabian—I haven't needed to.'
His hand moved into her thick, full hair, and

tightened in it, jerking her head back.

With a cry of pain, Megan had to look up at him. 'You're hurting!'

'Is Mark Bond your lover?' was all he said, still holding her by the hair.

'That's my business!' She was afraid to pull free in case he really hurt her, and that made her angrier. 'You big bully!' she muttered, glaring, and Dev let go of her but didn't move away, indeed moved closer and bent, his eyes fixed on her quivering mouth.

'Megan,' he whispered, and she ached to kiss him, watching his lips with bitter intensity.

Then the phone rang and they both jumped, eyes startled. Dev swore and swung away to snatch up the phone. 'Yes?' he roared into it and then scowled. 'Oh, yes, this is Devlin Hurst speaking.' His fury had quietened to a flat pretence of courtesy. 'Oh,' he said, listening. 'When? The weekend? Yes, certainly, tell Sir James I'd be delighted, thank him for me. Yes, yes, I'll pass that on, and I'm sure that will be OK. Thank you.' He put the phone down and turned an oddly speculative glance on Megan.

She was afraid he was about to start where he had left off, but instead he asked, 'Doing anything this weekend?'

She froze, hurriedly thinking. 'Yes, I'm visiting a friend,' she lied, when in fact she had nothing planned at all.

Blandly, Dev smiled at her. 'Then I'm afraid you must cancel it. That was Sir James Fordyce's secretary.'

'The chairman?' Megan had never even met the chairman of the board of directors of the company; indeed, she had never even set eyes on the man, although he was very famous, having been a very successful actor before he became a director and then one of the board of the television company. He had become chairman a few months ago, and so far hadn't made any changes in the direction the company had been taking for a long time, but everyone was expecting this new broom to start sweeping away some of the staff any day.

Megan was baffled. What had the chairman got to do with her, or indeed she to do with the chairman? Or his secretary, come to that?

'The chairman,' agreed Dev drily. 'His secretary rang to pass on his invitation for the weekend. He has a little place in Kent and wants us to join him there for a rather exclusive staff conference.'

'Oh,' Megan said, not quite taking it in. 'That should be fun for you . . . it was snowing in Kent, the last I heard.' Then she opened her eyes wide, shock in them. 'Us? Did you say us? What do you mean, us?'

'Us as in both of us,' said Dev. 'You and me, that's what I mean. What else could I mean?'

'I've never even met the chairman!'

'Now's your chance.'

'He doesn't know me, he can't do, we've never met!'

'I think you've established that,' Dev said solemnly. 'You and the chairman have never met, so far, but he wants to remedy that this weekend.'

Megan shook her head slowly, frowning. 'Why

should he? He can never have heard of me, why should he want to meet me?'

'Because I told him about you. He invited me and told me to bring my assistant, even though the last one looked like the Bride of Frankenstein, but I told him I had a new one and she looked like Snow White and he said in that case certainly bring her.'

She looked at him with slow disbelief, blue eyes angry. 'You can't have done, stop kidding.'

'No kidding,' he said, smiling. 'You are invited and you had better be there or the chairman is going to be disappointed, because he loves the story of Snow White too; maybe because he's a dwarf, and that is one part he wouldn't need to wear make-up for.'

Now she knew he was joking and she glared at him. 'Don't be ridiculous!'

Dev sat down again and pulled a notepad towards him. 'OK, the chairman isn't really a dwarf, just an actor, but the invitation is deadly serious, and you'll be there this weekend. It will be very good for your promotion prospects. In this business, it's not so much how good you are as who you know. Haven't you discovered that yet? Now stop distracting me. I must get down to some work.'

Indignantly, Megan said, 'I was not distracting you!'

'Oh, yes, you were,' he said, sliding her an insolent sideways look that made her face burn. 'Put the lights out and we'll either make love . . .' he watched her start to back, her eyes wary, and laughed, 'or we'll start the film,' he said in that soft, tormenting voice.

Megan's teeth were tight. He was enjoying this game of cat and mouse, but it was playing havoc with her nerves. Apparently oblivious of her anger, Dev picked up his scribbled notes and glanced over them, talking without looking at her. 'I'll see it through once, to decide which sections I'm going to use, and after that I want you to run down an old film for me—made some time in the Thirties, I think. I saw it once, years ago—it had some fascinating footage of the Manaus of the period; very grainy black and white newsreel film. I'd love to use a few feet of that for comparison with the Manaus of today.'

Megan groaned silently at the prospect of all the work involved in tracking down this piece of film; he probably didn't even know which studio had made it or who had directed it! But at least if Dev was watching his film footage he wouldn't be concentrating on her, so she crossed to the lights and switched them off, then drew up a chair to watch the film Dev himself had shot in the South American jungle. It was an unbearably vivid film, for her, because she was actually seeing what Dev had until now merely described to her: the heat, the insects, the snakes, the dark, impenetrable trees with their vines and creepers tangling the paths, and, of course, the river. That was always present, even when you couldn't see it, swirling with currents, running limpidly, flat and sullen, but always with that nightmarish quality which was unlike that of any river she had ever known, an air of threat.

Megan tried not to watch Dev all the time, but of course her eyes kept returning to the lean figure in a khaki cotton shirt and shorts, his black hair ruffled, his face daily growing more tanned. Perspiration trickled down his face, made his shirt stick to his body; under the tan she was sure his face was haggard, and his movements were often weary.

'Why do you all wear khaki?' she asked, after a while, and he grimaced.

'You can get very dirty in that jungle; mud, grass stains, sweat . . . you put something on in the morning and inside an hour it can be filthy. On the river you can wash clothes easily enough each evening and dry them on the boat, but white is out. It looks terrible after one or two washings. Khaki is the best colour, we found. It lasts longest.'

When they had run through the film once, Dev put on the lights and glanced at her. 'What do you think?'

'I can see you getting ill in front of my eyes,' she said without looking up.

'I was fine then!' He sounded taken aback. 'I didn't catch the bug until much later.'

'Maybe not, but it's obvious the climate was sapping your energy, and I'm not surprised. It looks terrible there.'

He shrugged. 'It isn't England, no, but I've been to South America before. I could handle the heat.'

'But you picked up a terrible disease!'

'That could have happened to anyone!'

'That's not my point!'

'What is your point, then?' he asked drily, his

eyes impatient.

'You shouldn't go back there!' she burst out, and then wished she hadn't when she saw the look in his face, the triumph smouldering in those grey eyes, the curve of satisfaction to his hard mouth.

'I thought you were indifferent to me, couldn't wait to get rid of me?' he purred, smiling.

Megan was so furious with herself she could have screamed. When would she learn to keep control over her stupid tongue? Hurriedly getting up, she almost ran to the door.

'I'll go and check out that old film,' she said huskily as she escaped, and was even angrier when she heard Dev laughing behind her, but he didn't try to stop her, or call her back. He had given her a difficult job to do; no doubt he realised how long it would take her to track the film down. She had so little to go on—just the subject matter and some vague idea of the period. Film libraries these days were very well catalogued and at least she had a starting point. She could check up on all the film shot in that part of the world during the relevant years, and fortunately it was not an area which had been much used in filming, so that the volume of film material was not as great as it would have been for some places.

She knew the various film libraries pretty well because she had had to use them from time to time for the Fabian show; she had contacts in them all. It was a big help to be on first-name terms with someone who was going to have to work very hard to help you, and she shamelessly sold them a picture of Dev as a remorseless slavedriver ready to tear her limb from limb if she didn't find the film he needed.

'I can't go back without it,' she moaned, rolling big blue eyes, and got immediate sympathy.

'I'll see what I can do,' they all promised and scurried off to search through dusty card indexes or tap their computer files. Megan spent the best part of the day looking for the film which matched Dev's patchy memory, and was about to go back empty-handed when someone came up with a rather poor copy of a film of an expedition along the Amazon. Dev had remembered it as grey and grainy. Since then it had deteriorated further; at times it was like seeing people through a pale pea soup, but Megan was sure she had located the right film.

'No, sorry, I can't possibly let you take the film,' she was told in an apologetic voice. 'More than my job's worth. Tell your ogre to come here and view it for himself, and if he still wants to use it some arrangement can probably be made with my own boss, but it will have to be official. It's quite a valuable piece of film, and it isn't in a good condition at all.'

'OK, thanks,' Megan said, relieved that she had managed to find the film at all. 'Mr Hurst will understand the situation.'

She found Dev in his office, frowning over a thick typed manuscript. Megan paused in the doorway, her heart missing a beat at the pallor and weariness she saw in his face. He hadn't noticed her yet, but he suddenly lifted his head and sighed, passing a hand over his eyes and yawning.

'You ought to be in bed,' Megan said, and he stiffened, looking round at her.

'Is that an offer?' his voice whispered smokily as he smiled at her.

She flushed angrily. 'Will you stop flirting with me?' How many times do I have to say it? It's . . .'

'Over!' he mocked. 'I know, you keep telling me—but somehow you aren't very convincing when you look at me like that, Megan.'

Her face was burning; she averted her eyes from his amused face. 'Oh, for God's sake!' she muttered. 'Can't you see I mean it, or are you so vain that you can't imagine any woman falling out of love with you?'

The silence which followed her outburst seemed to drag on for ever until she was on the verge of breaking down. She didn't dare to look at Dev; she was terrified of what she might see in his face. At last he said flatly, 'Well, did you get anywhere, hunting for the old film footage?'

Still not looking at him, and half sick with relief, she nodded. 'I think so. I've located a film that seemed a strong candidate, anyway, but it's in such poor condition that they wouldn't let me take it out of the library. You'll have to go and view it there, they said, and if it is what you want some sort of arrangement can be made, but it will have to go through official channels.'

'OK, I'll deal with that tomorrow, while you're going through my film again working with this script and looking at where I've marked possible cuts.'

She slowly went over to take the script from him. 'What is it?'

'I've had a typist working all day on the audio recording I brought back with me. I kept a taped diary; each evening before I went to sleep I recorded comments on what we'd done and seen, where we were on the journey, how far we had come and had to go, what film we had shot . . .' He lifted the heavy wadge of script and flicked the pages. 'This is it! The girl did a very good job; there aren't many errors and most of those are in place-names or people's names.' He handed it to Megan, drily saying, 'Careful! It's heavy.'

He wasn't exaggerating; her arm sagged under the weight of it. 'This isn't the script of the actual film, then?'

He shook his head. 'No, but I talked about each section of the journey, and so I've used this to work out a schedule for the actual programme. Working from this damn great thing we can type out a running list and then I'll put together a working script.'

She nodded. 'I see. OK, I'll do that tomorrow, then.' She looked at her watch. 'It's late, I must go.'

'Got a date?'

'Yes,' she lied, walking away, and Dev let her go without another word. Maybe at last he had got the message? she thought, and felt bleakly resigned as she made her way home to her silent, empty, lonely flat. She ate a light salad supper in the kitchen then sat down to watch a rival chat show with a comedian host. Johnny liked them to watch it each week, to keep track of what the other man was doing, and tonight Megan was startled to see Mark on the show. That would amuse Johnny; he loved it when someone he had discovered got picked up by a rival show! The camera focused on Mark's face as he smiled, and she sighed, frowning. She hadn't seen him since the night he'd had the fight with Dev. She should have rung him, written, perhaps—but she simply didn't know what to say and so it had seemed easier not to say anything. Sometimes silence was much wiser.

In the morning, she arrived at the office early and started work on the typed manuscript of Dev's diary. He didn't show up for hours and Megan became utterly absorbed in what she was reading and hearing: Dev's words, Dev's voice, Dev's mind. She hardly noticed the passage of time. What she was doing was far too important for time to matter.

She had known Dev for such a short time before he went away, and she really hadn't known him very well. She had fallen in love with her senses; she had wanted him with painful intensity, but she hadn't found out much about the human being inside the body she desired. A hot flush crawled up her cheeks as that dawned on her. She hadn't realised all this until now, because she had been mistaking naked desire for love.

Dev hadn't helped, of course—he hadn't told her anything about himself; indeed, he had hidden far too much. Now she was beginning to know him. In this copious diary he had recorded everything in a stream-of-consciousness style, putting down whatever came into his head— plants he had noticed and filmed, flowers and ferns and trees, butterflies and moths, ants and termites, birds, toads, snakes, lizards, monkeys and wild cats. Dev seemed to forget nothing, but there was far more to the diary than the fauna and flora he noticed. That was not what fascinated Megan.

It was the insight she was being given into Dev himself—the way he thought, his motives and dreams, what gave him that drive and energy. Perhaps because he was so far away from everything familiar, or because each day he used up all his energy and was half asleep when he began to record, or maybe because after a while he was falling ill, Dev began to be amazingly frank on the tapes. At first, he had been more concerned with mundane stuff like the exact day, weather, distance travelled, what he had done or seen. But then he changed; almost as though he was using the tapes as a confessional, a doctor's couch. He talked about why he had always been fascinated by the Amazon; one of the last unknown places of the earth, he said, a place of secrets and mystery, darkness and untamed nature. It would vanish before too long if something wasn't done to save it, and Dev had wanted to see it before it was too late. It was ephemeral, finite, like everything else, he said.

That was the thread running through everything he said; the ephemeral nature of life. He talked grimly about death, in the jungle, on the river,

how abruptly it could come, without warning, the
way it had to a friend who had died suddenly in
his teens, then mentioned his mother's death
while he was still at school, how that had affected
him and then he said something about Gianna.
Oh, he didn't name her, of course; it was just a
brief, sideways comment about women who
walked out on you, betrayed you. 'Sex is a little
death, of course,' he said. 'Isn't that because even
while you're in heaven, you know that hell is just
around the corner?'

Megan knew he was talking about Gianna; who
else could it be? That icy, bitter tone of voice was
painful to listen to—who else but Gianna would he
hate so much?

She closed her eyes, her hands over her face.
Not me, she thought. He doesn't mean me! Or did
he?

It was hard to guess from the diary so far,
because, although he talked about his own
thoughts and feelings, he never mentioned names
or personal events. These were very impersonal
admissions; journeys through his mind rather
than private gossip, and the occasional mention of
someone else was always discreetly veiled. Dev
knew very well that his were not the only pair of
eyes that would read his diary; he was very careful
what and how he wrote.

Had her letter arrived by the time he wrote that
passage, though? She read it over again, brow
furrowed, but couldn't tell. She thought back over
everything that had happened since he came back.
Did he hate her? His passion could be violent;

almost volcanic—but desire could spring from hatred too, couldn't it?

She sighed bleakly. Yes, you could hate and desire at the same time; sometimes when Dev was cruel to her she hated him, but she wanted him badly, too.

'Problems?' his deep voice said behind her at that second, and she swung round, her heart missing a beat.

'No . . . not really,' she stammered.

He walked towards her and she felt her face burning. Dev noticed it, too, his grey eyes narrowing.

'So how's it coming?' He perched on the edge of her desk, his leg brushing hers in a casual way, and Megan carefully shifted a fraction to avoid the contact. She wasn't looking at Dev, but she felt him stiffen, felt the sideways glance she got.

'Fine. I'm almost finished, I'll have that running list ready as soon as I can type it up.'

He leaned forward to peer over her shoulder at the script open on the desk. She could hardly breath as she felt his cheek almost touching hers.

'That's great,' he said softly, his arm encircling her. It was deliberate, she knew that. Dev was forcing the little intimacies on her, aware of her reactions, daring her to stop him. It was coat-trailing of a provocative kind, and Megan could have hit him.

She swung her chair sideways so that she could get up without touching him, but Dev moved too. As she stood up she found him in front of her, looking her up and down with speculative mockery.

'Something bothering you?' he drawled, watching her hot face with satisfaction.

All Megan could do was snap, 'No! I'm just going to make myself some coffee—want some?' and walk away, resisting the temptation to run.

That was what it was like all that week. Working with Dev at such close quarters made walking barefoot over hot coals look quite an attractive proposition! He went out of his way to make it hard for her, of course. The way he watched her made it impossible for her to forget that they were alone, and he never missed a chance of touching her, standing close to her, making her aware of him. Her nerves leapt every time he came within a foot of her, and she found it hard to concentrate.

She couldn't even be consistent; she hated him for doing this to her, but every time she saw him her heart turned over. She kept telling herself she couldn't stand it, yet she dreaded the time when it must end.

CHAPTER EIGHT

SHE was even more on edge over the coming
weekend. Why had the chairman invited her? Or
had he simply asked Dev to bring a girl? Megan
wished she had the nerve to refuse to go, but she
knew that it would be crazy to pass up a chance to
meet the chairman and his influential friends!
Dev was right, her career could get quite a boost
from spending time with such important people,
but Megan wished Dev wasn't going to be there.
When it came down to it, it was Dev she was
really worrying about. It was bad enough
spending all day with him in that office—being
with him all weekend under the same roof was
going to be a terrible strain.

Dev drove her down there, saying very little at
first, and Megan sat staring straight ahead,
deeply aware of him sitting there beside her. He
was wearing a dark grey suit which made him
look thinner and rather pale. His red-striped shirt
and dark red silk tie emphasised the formal look
of the suit. Dev was out to impress, she
thought—the chairman? Gossips in the canteen
kept hinting that Dev was in line for a very
important executive job, high up in the
company—was it all smoke, or was there fire
behind that rumour?

'Is it a big party this weekend?' she asked, and

Dev shrugged.

'I doubt it.'

'Any special reason why he's asked you? Is it to hear all about the Amazon trip?'

'No,' he coolly admitted. 'He wants to talk me into taking a job.'

So for once the gossips had been right! Megan gave him a wary, sidelong look. 'In London?'

He nodded. 'But I'd have to take it up immediately, I can't ask him to wait another year until I've finished the Amazon project. He wants me to hand that over to my assistant and take up this other job at once.'

Her throat hurt and she was pale. 'Will you?' she asked huskily.

He shrugged again. 'I don't think so.'

She bit her lower lip, knowing it was none of her business any more, she had no right to comment or even care, and anyway, it would be easier for her if he wasn't always around—and yet deeply afraid of what might happen if he went back to the Amazon.

'Is it a good job?'

'Very.' He was curt, indifferent.

'Is it wise to pass up a chance like that?'

He suddenly swung the wheel and pulled off the road into a leafy lay-by and Megan's throat began to beat with a frantic pulse as he parked and turned to face her.

'What are you doing?'

His grey eyes were glittering with some fierce emotion. Hate or love? she wondered, unable to look away from the heat of his stare. It was like looking into the sun; it blinded her and yet she couldn't stop.

'Give me a reason for staying, Megan,' he said thickly, and she had never felt such pain, because she wanted so much to give him that reason, to beg him to stay, for her sake, and yet she couldn't do that because if she married him she would be bringing him another sort of unhappiness. She stared at him like a dumb animal, cornered and helpless, shaking and close to tears; and Dev waited and watched her, the glitter in his eyes like the lance of a laser now, and it was hate she saw, not love, but there was nothing she could do.

'I'm sorry,' she whispered, and Dev's teeth met, his lip curled back from them in a silent snarl.

He reached out for her with hands that hurt and meant to, and she writhed and fought as silently, trying to keep her mouth closed to him, trying to control the hungry leap of her senses as he touched her. She had never in her life felt such sensual torment; her flesh was melting with the heat inside her body, she was weak with bitter yearning, yet she struggled not to give in to it—struggled not with Dev, but with herself, because she knew she was the real enemy. She knew she couldn't have Dev, it was impossible, forbidden, but she wanted him more now than she had ever had.

At last Dev stopped, gave up, released her, still in the same angry silence, and as he put his foot down with a roar of acceleration, and shot back on to the main road, she turned her head away from him and let the tears trickle out from under her closed lids.

Why on earth had she come? Hadn't she known how it would be if she spent the weekend with him in the country, even at the chairman's house? It was going to be the worst ordeal of her life!

As they shot up the drive towards the place, she pretended to cough, in order to have the excuse for getting out a handkerchief and blowing her nose, managing at the same time to dry her eyes.

She only noticed the house as she was getting out of the car; it was large and imposing, set among perfectly stylised gardens with manicured lawns and beautifully shaped box and yew trees. She saw a soft white blur under some trees; snowdrops, she thought, frowning. It was nearly spring; soon the daffodils would come, taking the winds of March with beauty, and by then Dev would be on his way back to South America.

The chairman himself appeared, all smiles. He was a charming man; smoothly practised in the art of making people like him, putting them at their ease.

'Delighted to meet you, Megan,' he said, holding her hands and gazing at her with apparent admiration.

'Thank you for inviting me,' she said, aware of Dev watching them.

'Thank you for coming,' said the chairman, bland as custard. 'Come in out of this cold weather.'

I wish I could, she thought, following him into the hall, but the weather of her life was far colder than the chilly February day.

His house was glossy and perfect, like himself; not quite genuine, like himself; all things to all men, like himself. Megan viewed it with a jaundiced eye; ready to be critical of everything she saw because she wished she was somewhere else. She was whisked up to her room and told to ring if she wanted anything; the housekeeper would look after her. Megan smiled until her face ached, and when she was alone she sat down on the chintz-draped bed in the pretty, chintzy bedroom, and hated her surroundings.

There were quite a few people staying in the house; mostly company executives and their wives. The men she found boring, the women clannish—they all knew each other already and, although they were not unfriendly, they weren't precisely friendly, either. She got the impression they weren't sure yet if she mattered. If she had been going to marry Dev, they might have been more interested in her, or if Dev had publicly accepted a job on the administrative level, that might have given her status, but as it was she found herself more or less ignored while they talked about clothes, their husband's work, new curtains, their husband's promotion and salary rise, the cost of petrol, the size of their husband's desk, and so on . . .

The chairman was charming to them all; particularly the women, for them he had a special brand of charm which meant gazing into their eyes, holding their hands and calling them honey or lovely. He never used their names, probably because he never remembered them. He looked as if he had trouble remembering his own, but to Megan's surprise, that Saturday afternoon, while his wife was showing everyone else around the vast Victorian conservatories, the chairman hijacked her from the party and took her off alone with him.

'Come and see my etchings,' he purred, and when she laughed said, 'I mean it! It's such a corny line that I simply had to learn how to etch.'

They had been framed and hung in a line on a stark white wall; all nature studies, black and white and very striking.

Megan admired them without needing to lie, and the chairman beamed on her.

'They aren't bad, are they? I should have been an artist, not an actor. I was a competent actor, but I would have been a happier painter.'

Megan smiled politely, wondering why he had really brought her here alone. She hoped he wasn't going to make a pass at her. She didn't feel up to coping with a crisis of that sort today.

Suddenly he said, 'Did you know about this job we've offered Dev?'

Megan started, her blue eyes wide and her face pale between her soft, dark hair. She nodded silently after a second, aware of the chairman watching her.

'Why has he turned it down?' he asked brusquely, and she took a sharp breath.

'Has he?' It wasn't a surprise, but it still shook her, and her face whitened still further.

'He didn't tell you that?'

She shook her head, and the chairman frowned at her.

'But you're the reason why he refused it?'

The question was like a knife in her flesh; she looked away, fighting for control, and couldn't answer.

'Talk to him,' the chairman said, after a moment. 'I won't ask any more questions. I don't want to pry into personal matters, but I've had a report on his health and this tropical medicine specialist he's been seeing is concerned about him: Dev shouldn't go back to the Amazon, at least until he has fully recovered, and he's still pretty weak, I'm told. See what you can do, there's a good girl. Surely whatever's wrong between you can be worked out?'

Megan said huskily; 'I'll try to talk to him, but I can't . . . I can't promise anything else . . .'

Dev was with the rest of the party in the conservatories, admiring the ferns and begonias, the hyacinths and hothouse tulips, but as Megan joined them the chairman's wife gave her a quick, shrewd look, and said, 'Look at the time! I think I'll go and have a bath before dinner. How about you, ladies?'

The guests drifted off in her wake, but Dev, his dark brows together, had noticed the way his hostess had looked at Megan. He sat down on a pink velvet-covered love-seat, carefully arranged among the scented flowers.

'Aren't you going to take a bath and dress before dinner?' he asked her, and Megan wandered about, pretending to look at the potted plants.

'In a minute—these blue hyacinths have a very strong scent, don't they?'

'What did the chairman want?' Dev asked curtly. 'Or can I guess? Don't bother to say whatever he told you to say. I'm not interested.'

She swung round, blue eyes distressed. 'Dev, take that job! Don't risk your life again.'

'Don't pretend you give a damn what I do!' His lips barely moved, his voice was icy, but his eyes were molten steel: white-hot and dangerous.

That question must not be answered, so she said miserably, 'Nothing is worth risking your life for!'

'Well, you certainly aren't!' he muttered, and she flinched, meeting the hatred in his stare.

Shaking, she turned and ran, not caring now if he realised she was running away from him. In her room she sat there for a long time, cold and miserable, then she showered quickly and began to dress. She was in her white lace bra and panties when Dev walked in and she swung round, crimson and furious.

'Get out of here, Dev!'

'You forgot to lock your door!' was all he said, staring, and the glitter of his eyes made her heart beat heavily, her breathing thicken.

'Don't, Dev,' she whispered, suddenly paralysed.

He took a step towards her, his grey eyes seeming to burn her skin as he stared at her. Why hadn't she remembered to lock her door? She had known he might follow her, hadn't she? A Freudian slip, she thought.

'A Freudian slip,' Dev said hoarsely, and her

eyes flickered in shock. They were beginning to think alike after all these hours alone together!

'Why, Megan?' he said, his hands sliding down her bare arms, pulling her closer. 'Did you want me to find you like this?'

Shame made her look down; was that what she had wanted? She didn't know, and that was worrying—was her unconscious operating so shamelessly on its own?

He softly cupped her breast and a piercing excitement made her dizzy; she closed her eyes and Dev breathed faster, one arm round her, his hand splayed on her bare back. His mouth was hot; she tried vainly not to respond, but she needed the touch of his lips, the intimacy that had threatened her all that week in the office when they were so close and yet hadn't kissed, hadn't been in each other's arms. It had been on their minds all the time, though. Desire had been in the air they breathed; it had fountained inside her and driven her mad with frustration.

His hands moved and left a track of fire everywhere they touched, and Megan had to touch him, too. He groaned as she did, then suddenly picked her up and carried her to the bed, his mouth burrowing between her breasts.

'No, Dev,' she gasped, surfacing in shock.

'Yes,' he muttered, caressing her naked body with shaking hands. 'I want you so badly I'm going crazy.'

She wanted him too, but she had to stop him before it was too late. 'You aren't making love to me, Dev,' she said, turning her head aside and pushing at his shoulders. 'I won't let you; do I have to make a scene to stop you? If I scream the whole house will hear me.'

He lifted his head, face dark red, those grey eyes hot and raging. 'You little bitch! What sort of games are you playing? You let me go so far and then call a halt, is that it? Just when I'm almost out of my mind? Is that what turns you on—not sex, but teasing a man and then watching him go mad with frustration? Do you know what men call a woman like you?'

His voice made her sick, but she was angry, too. How dared he say such things to her? She hit him hard, across the face, and Dev looked shocked, sitting up, a hand to the livid mark on his cheek.

Megan rolled off the bed, grabbed a dressing-gown and ran for the bathroom. She locked herself into it and wouldn't emerge until she was sure Dev had gone.

She didn't have long to wait; she heard the angry slam of her bedroom door and his striding footsteps, and when everything was quiet again she crept out, shaking.

How was she going to stand the next twenty-four hours? Every time she was near Dev she was going to be on tenterhooks, yet she dared not leave.

Slowly, with trembling fingers, she continued dressing, did her hair and make-up, looked bleakly at her reflection and then in the mirror saw the crumpled bed, the indentations that their bodies had made.

Shuddering, she swung round and pulled off the cover, shook it and remade the bed, erasing all evidence of what had happened, but she couldn't wipe the memory from her own mind, and, when she went downstairs to dinner and found Dev talking to the other guests, she knew it was there, in his mind, too. He gave her a glance icy and remote—and she went to talk to one of the other women, struggling to keep a calm expression on her face.

It was a dreadful evening, and she went to bed early, but lay awake wondering how she was going to get through the next day. To her enormous relief, the chairman chose to hold a conference with his executives throughout the morning, and Dev sat in on it, leaving the women to their own devices. Megan chatted and walked through the gardens and, on closer acquaintance, got on well enough with the chairman's wife.

For the rest of that long, long day she managed to be surrounded by people whenever she saw Dev, but he would be driving her back to London and she could not escape him then. She need not have worried; he did drive her, but he was in a grim, silent mood. He didn't say a word until he dropped her at her flat.

As she got out, he said curtly, 'As we've done all the work necessary for my programme, you might as well go back to Fabian's office tomorrow.'

Megan gave him a quick, startled look, but before she could react he had leaned over, closed his car door and driven away, leaving her on the pavement, staring after him.

Dev had given up, she realised, her face chill and unhappy. It really was over now; he had accepted her decision.

CHAPTER NINE

'YOU'RE in the wrong office!' joked Johnny when he saw her, and she pretended to smile as she explained. 'I see,' Johnny said. 'He got bored and threw you back to me, did he? Well, I've got plenty for you to do, haven't we, Fanny?'

'Pronouns a bit mixed today, aren't they?' Fanny said. 'But we're glad to have you back, Megan. Look, could you ring this lady for me and find out how many films she has made? All the reference books give different figures.'

They were all too busy to care about what had happened between her and Dev, and she meant to push all thought of Dev out of her head, but then Johnny dropped another bombshell half-way through the week.

'By the way, Hurst will be on the next show,' he said, and watched her shaken face with interest. 'Mind you, he wasn't too keen, said he couldn't do it at first, but the chairman spoke to him. I gather he has finished putting his Amazon programme together now, and the chairman wants us to talk about that. They're going to put it out quite soon.'

Megan was dry-mouthed, and could only nod.

'Ring him and check that he'll be there, on the day, won't you?' said Johnny, and then walked off before she could plead an excuse. She was as nervous as a kitten after that, and on the morning of the next show she nerved herself to ring Dev, but he was out. She left a message on his answering machine, then spent the day fretting that he wouldn't turn up for the programme. When Johnny grabbed hold of her, though, and demanded, 'He will be there?' she immediately tried to look confident and nodded, because there was no point in making Johnny edgy, too.

'Of course!'

'Great. Got my briefing ready?'

'I'm just typing it now.'

'Well, get on with it. Why are you standing around chatting?'

She didn't bother to point out that she had been sitting at her desk working on her VDU when he'd pulled her out of her chair.

'Yes, Johnny,' she said soothingly, because it was always the same. As each show approached Johnny grew more and more paranoid. He was the lynchpin of the programme; it stood or fell by him and everyone remembered that when he started falling apart or bawled them out over nothing.

She was in the green room before they went on the air, handing out frivolous snippets of food or glasses of cheap wine to the guests, who looked askance at their glasses after one sip. 'What is this stuff?' asked one. 'Paint-stripper?'

'Sorry,' she said, smiling politely, although it was an effort to smile at all while she was on edge over Dev.

'Get me some whisky, there's a good girl,' said a famous actor, sweat on his forehead. 'I hate first nights.'

She laughed, although he wasn't really being funny, just suffering from nerves in spite of all his years in the theatre. Television was quite another medium, one he was unfamiliar with; they had had a tough time talking him on to the show and Johnny had been afraid he wouldn't arrive, but then Johnny was always afraid his stars wouldn't show up!

There was a flurry at the door, and Megan tensed, her antennae picking up Dev's presence in the room. She smiled vaguely at the famous actor. 'Yes, of course, I won't be a moment.'

She walked over to the drinks table, fighting not to look in Dev's direction. He was being hailed by Fanny; she would get him a drink. Megan picked up the whisky and poured some into a glass, her hand shaking.

'Hey! You trying to get someone drunk?' asked one of the other researchers, looking amused.

Megan realised then what a stiff drink she had poured and grimaced. 'It's for Aidan.'

'Oh! Right!' the other girl said, grinning with understanding, but Fanny overheard and swung round, frowning.

'That man is not getting drunk and wrecking my show! Pour that back into the bottle, Megan, then go and look after Dev Hurst. He's on last.'

Megan swallowed, her mouth very dry, but managed to force a smile. 'He doesn't need a babysitter, he's an old hand,' she said huskily.

'He seems odd this time,' Fanny shrugged. 'When he was on before, he took it in his stride, I remember. Maybe it's his illness, or perhaps I'm imagining it, but he seems different, so keep an eye on him, will you?' She had been muttering as they crossed the room, but as they came up to Dev she raised her voice and said, 'Sorry to love and leave you, but I have a lot to do before airtime, Dev. You know Megan, don't you?'

She vanished, leaving them staring at each other in silence.

'Do I know you?' Dev asked pointedly. He was wearing a dark city suit and white shirt; the formal clothes made him look thinner than ever, his brown skin only emphasising the haggard tautness of his face. He didn't smile at Megan; he just considered her with hostility glittering in his grey eyes.

'Can I get you another drink?' she asked, pretending not to have heard the biting sarcasm.

'No, thanks. You haven't driven me to drink yet.' He looked her over insultingly. 'Very demure; butter-wouldn't-melt-in-your-mouth time, is it?'

Megan looked desperately at her watch. Only a little longer and she could escape from this.

'I'd love to know what really makes you tick,' Dev muttered in a low voice. There were people all round them and she was relieved he wasn't making this a more public scene, but any minute now he might.

'Shall we go, people?' Fanny said from the door and then they heard the laughter and clapping from the audience. The warm-up man was getting them into the right mood before Johnny came on.

The famous actor strolled after Fanny; he was the first guest that night because he was appearing in a new play and would have to be driven across London in time for curtain up. Dev turned to go, too.

'Not yet,' Megan said, huskily. 'You're the last on—another twenty minutes to wait, I'm afraid. We can watch the programme, though.'

The green room had a monitor hanging in one corner; a giant screen on which Johnny's face now appeared, magnified and dominating. The audience whistled and clapped and Johnny beamed.

'Fool!' muttered Dev, and walked away to the window where he stood staring down into the street at the distant lights and cars. On the screen the faces talked; the applause sounded like the meaningless wash of the sea backwards and forwards on an empty beach. Johnny grimaced and winked and the actor preened, stroking back a thinning lock of hair. Megan watched Dev's back and wished she was somewhere else, then thought how stupid she was being because she would rather stand there watching Dev, even knowing he now hated her, than be unable to see him at all.

Dev's call came and he went out without so much as a glance at her. She watched the monitor during the interview and now the talk was not just a pointless buzz; she really listened. Johnny had to work harder than he had on the last interview with Dev; he had a rather puzzled air, even though he smiled as much. What was wrong? his eyes asked, and he sweated in case the interview might go disastrously awry.

'So, are you back home for good or . . .'

'No, I'm flying back to the Amazon tomorrow,' Dev said, and Megan jerked in shock, her blue eyes darkening. Johnny was startled, too; in fact his jaw dropped, because she hadn't had that little titbit in the notes she had typed out for him.

'You're going tomorrow?' Johnny pretended to find it all hilarious, laughing loudly. 'Why wasn't I told? Nobody tells me anything.'

Megan was going to be hauled over the coals next time he saw her, but that didn't matter. The only thing that mattered was that Dev was going back to the Amazon. Her eyes focused on his thin, fleshless features. He wasn't well enough yet. It was stupid, reckless, crazy. He couldn't be serious; what about the tests he was supposed to be having? Had he told the specialist he was seeing? He hadn't been back long and he had said he was staying for some weeks.

'Why the sudden change of plan?' asked Johnny for her, as if their minds had been moving on the same track.

Dev shrugged. 'I'm eager to get on with my filming, and I'm more or less back to normal, health-wise.' He was flat and offhand, but Johnny scented a mystery, a secret, and his eyes glinted. He tried to ferret it out of Dev, using all his charm, his expertise as an interviewer, but he got nowhere, and while he was still prying away at the locked door of Dev's secrecy the music came up and the credits rolled, and Johnny, with an irritated smile, began talking them out, thanking everyone, saying, 'See you same time, same channel, Thursday . . . don't be late, now . . .'

They were off the air and Johnny erupted into the room a few moments later, fire and brimstone spewing from him.

'What the hell went wrong? Why didn't you mention that he was going back that soon? What do you think I pay you for?'

'He didn't tell me!' Megan was talking like an automaton, her eyes on the door. Was Dev coming back in here? 'I'm sorry, Johnny, I had no idea . . .'

'The whole interview was the wrong way round because I didn't know that one thing! If I'd known I would have asked different questions.'

'It isn't her fault,' Fanny soothed, joining them. 'And, anyway, Johnny love, it was a nice surprise, coming out of the blue like that.' I didn't see anything about it in the Press beforehand, so we had a little scoop. It will be in the papers tomorrow that he announced it out of the blue on the Fabian show, and that is always good publicity for us, isn't it?'

Sulkily Johnny agreed. 'But I don't like being caught out like that; it makes me panic. You know how I hate to improvise.'

Fanny patted his cheek. 'Lovely, you were wonderful, wasn't he, Megan? Rose to it magnificently; not a hair out of place and asked all the right things, gave all the right reactions. Couldn't fault you, honestly.'

Johnny purred. 'Really? You aren't just saying

that?'

'Really,' said Fanny, and Johnny went happily off to have a drink before he left. Fanny looked at Megan and winked.

'I'm sorry to fall down on that one,' Megan said flatly.

'Not to worry, love. I gather Devlin Hurst can be a difficult guy. He may have held the bombshell back deliberately. It had more impact that way. Johnny looked so taken aback! It was obvious he really didn't know.'

'Has he left?' asked Megan, and Fanny looked blank.

'Who?'

'Devlin Hurst.'

'I think he has—walked off without a word. He's a surly devil at times, isn't he?'

Megan laughed humourlessly. 'Yes, you could say that. Excuse me, Fanny . . . I have to rush . . .'

She reached the car park just in time to see Dev drive away, and slowed, biting her lip. What had she chased down here for, anyway? It was all over. They had said their goodbyes and it would be foolish to see him again. It wasn't her business if he chose to return to the Amazon. What had she been intending to say to him, if she had caught up with him?

She walked over to her own car and got behind the wheel, but sat there for several minutes to pull herself together before she tried to drive. Her mind was shot to pieces—she didn't want to be a danger to other drivers.

She had only been home for half an hour when

the doorbell went. For some reason she leapt to the conclusion that it was Dev and ran to answer it, her loose white lounging robe flying around her, but to her disbelief she found herself facing his sister, Emma Stansfield.

'Is he here?' Emma burst out, and Megan dumbly shook her head. Emma gave her a hostile survey from her tousled hair down over the white robe. 'I don't believe you,' she said, and pushed past Megan calling her brother's name. 'Dev! Dev!'

Megan followed her, closing the front door. Emma looked into the kitchen and then into the sitting-room before heading purposefully towards the bedroom.

'Where do you think you're going?' Megan tried to stop her and was pushed aside.

'I saw that stupid programme you work for! I know he's talking about going back there tomorrow and he can't. It could kill him.' Emma hurled the words over her shoulder as she pulled the bedroom door open. 'Dev! I've got to talk to . . .' Her voice trailed away.

'He isn't here,' Megan repeated flatly.

'Then where is he?' Emma's hands curled into fists at her sides, as if she wanted to hit somebody. Me, most likely! thought Megan. Emma had made no secret of the fact that she disliked her.

'You've tried his flat?'

'Of course I have!' snapped Emma, scowling. 'Do you think I'm stupid?'

Megan felt like answering that, and Emma read as much in her eyes. She stared back, her curved red mouth furious, then let out a groan.

'Oh, maybe I am! Did you know he was going back tomorrow?'

Megan shook her head.

'Can't you talk him out of it?' his sister demanded, glaring.

Megan shook her head again.

'He's supposed to be going to marry you! Haven't you got any influence over him?' Emma used a sneering voice, ran her scornful eyes over Megan again.

'None,' Megan said. 'And we aren't getting married now. It's all over, you'll be relieved to hear!'

Emma looked taken aback, her pale eyes fixed on Megan's face. 'He came to his senses, did he? Well, that's something, I suppose.' She walked back to the front door and Megan escorted her without saying anything, but instead of leaving Emma suddenly stopped and burst out, 'What happened, anyway? Why did he break off the engagement? I saw him a few days ago, and he didn't mention it.'

'Perhaps he didn't want to talk about it!' Megan said coolly, and his sister shook her head.

'He talked about you! He said he was going into the country for the weekend with you; but he didn't breathe a word about the marriage being off.'

Megan winced at that, realising that Dev had been refusing to believe she was serious about not marrying him.

Emma Stansfield watched her intently, her face tight with suspicion. 'Did he catch you with someone else?' she abruptly accused.

'No, he did not!' Megan muttered, flushing darkly.

'Then why do you look so guilty?' Emma ran a shaking hand through her immaculately styled hair. 'My God, it's happened again!'

'What has?' Megan was bewildered.

Emma's eyes were angrily contemptuous; they were worried, too. 'Poor Dev, no wonder he's decided to go back to South America right away. It almost broke him into little pieces the last time—when Gianna ran out on him! He took years to get over it and he was scared stiff of getting involved with anyone else in case it happened again.' She saw Megan frowning and snapped at her, 'Don't tell me you didn't know all about it, because I remember it being mentioned on that stupid programme. Johnny Fabian asked Dev about Gianna and Dev changed the subject.'

Megan remembered that, too. She had seen the veiled look on Dev's face, the coldness in his eyes as he talked about something else. Johnny hadn't been surprised; he was used to famous people changing the subject if he ventured on to delicate ground. He rarely pursued the matter; that was not the name of the game on the Fabian show. It was far too cosy, too warm and light-hearted. Their viewers did not want to see Johnny going for the jugular. They wanted to watch with a smile, and Johnny was far too shrewd not to give them what they wanted.

'Gianna was so beautiful, that was the trouble,' said Emma. 'Too many other men were chasing her, and the one who got her was ten times richer than Dev. It was his money that she wanted, and Dev knew it. Why else do you think he ever settled for you? Because you weren't pretty and he didn't need to be afraid of losing you to someone else.'

Megan held the door open, her mouth a stiff white line. 'Would you go now, please? You've insulted me enough, don't you think?'

'I couldn't do that! Why, I've barely scratched the surface. If I told you what I think of you I'd be here all day.'

'Just go!'

'If Dev dies out there, I swear I'll come back here and kill you!' Emma hissed, and Megan lost her head.

'If he dies, you'll be welcome to kill me.'

Emma's grey eyes narrowed; for a brief instant she looked so like Dev that Megan did a double-take. 'You sound as if you mean that!'

'I do,' Megan said hoarsely, then felt like biting out her tongue, because she had not meant to blurt out the truth to Emma, who might repeat everything she said to Dev.

'If you feel like that about him, why is the marriage off? Did Dev jilt you? Or was it the other way around?'

Megan closed her eyes for a second, then looked stubbornly at the other woman. 'Look, I'm tired. I've had a bad day. Will you please go away? There's no point in talking about it any more.'

'I wish I understood all this,' Emma said, then stopped talking as someone else loomed up behind her. She looked round to stare. It was Mark

Bond, in evening dress, looking very elegant. Emma gave Megan a sarcastic look. 'Is he the part of the puzzle that you neglected to mention?'

Megan had had enough. She turned and walked into the sitting-room and a moment later heard the front door close. She didn't look round as Mark joined her, but said wearily, 'I'm sorry, Mark, but I can't talk now.'

'I saw the show tonight—so Hurst is going back to the Amazon? Does that mean it's finished, you and him?'

'Oh, please, Mark!' she groaned, putting her hands over her face to hide the slow tears escaping from her lashes.

'Megan! For heaven's sake!' He put his arms around her tightly and she couldn't break free; she shut her eyes and leaned on him, sobbing soundlessly, her whole body shaking.

When she had stopped crying he wiped her wet face with a clean handkerchief and made her sit down while he poured her a stiff drink from a bottle of whisky she had on hand for friends arriving unexpectedly. She didn't like it, herself, and tried to refuse it, but he held it to her lips and insisted she drank some.

Sitting beside her afterwards, he held her hand tightly, watching her. 'What's this all about, Megan? Don't you think I'm owed some sort of explanation?'

She gave him a rueful glance, shaking her head.

'Now, come on, Megan, you aren't the type to burst into tears over nothing at all!'

She grimaced at him. 'Right, I'm the tough-guy

type.'

He smiled at her with sudden tenderness. 'I wouldn't say that, exactly, but you are very inhibited.'

'Inhibited?' She went pink and he laughed.

'A dirty word, huh? I wasn't talking about sex, although I would, given any encouragement . . .?' He slid a wicked, sideways glance and she shook her head at him. Mark heaved a dramatic sigh. 'Too bad, but anyway, what I meant was that you find it hard to talk about yourself, you're secretive, shy, especially where your feelings are concerned. I've known you for months now, but you're still something of a mystery to me. But I still like you, inhibited or otherwise, so if you do ever need a shoulder to cry on, I've got two!'

She laughed shakily. 'Thanks, Mark.'

'You know I fancy you like mad,' he said ruefully, 'and I'd thought I was getting somewhere with you, only then Hurst came back, and when I realised you'd stood me up for him, and lied to me about it I lost my temper.'

She nodded without answering.

He grimaced. 'Yeah, I remember it well, too! He beat the hell out of me, and I deserved it, after what I'd said to you!'

She couldn't help laughing at his droll tone, but she knew him well enough to realise that Mark hated admitting to her that Dev had won that fight. He was proud of his muscularity and fitness; it must really stick in his throat that Dev had beaten him, and she admired him for talking about it so frankly.

'You had provocation,' she comforted, smiling at him. 'I'm sorry if I hurt you. I like you, too, Mark, but . . . well, I met Dev first, I'm afraid.'

He nodded, frowning. 'Megan, tell me about you and Hurst—that was his sister, Graham Stansfield's wife, wasn't it? What was she doing here? I got the impression the two of you were having a row. Is she at the root of whatever is wrong?' His eyes were gentle. 'Come on, you can trust me, Megan!'

He was right; she needed to talk to someone or she would go mad, so she slowly said, 'You remember the accident I had?'

He looked surprised. 'Yes, of course.'

'There was more to it than I've told you,' she said huskily. 'They had to operate immediately I reached the hospital. I was very badly injured and I didn't really know anything about what was happening to me. When I did start taking notice, they didn't tell me for a long time that the worst of my injuries wasn't something anyone could see.' Taking a deep breath, she muttered,' They had to remove my womb, Mark. I can't have babies.'

Mark made a thick sound of shocked incredulity and, worse, of pity. 'Megan! My God!' He looked down, frowning and very pale. 'I don't know what to say; you poor kid, what rotten luck.'

She nodded. 'I'm getting used to it now, but at first it was almost more than I could bear, and there was something else . . . you see, Dev had asked me to marry him.'

Mark sucked in breath, staring at her. She wished he wouldn't; it was hard enough to talk about all this without feeling his horrified, compassionate eyes on her face.

'Was this before he went to South America, or . . .'

'I crashed my car on the way back from the airport the day he left.' She suddenly remembered the pain of those moments, watching Dev walk away through the barrier after icily ignoring her. Mark had confessed that he had been jealous of her and Dev—but his feelings were mild compared to Dev's jealousy. What had happened to Dev years ago, with Gianna Montesi, had made him the man he was today—or had he already been a violently jealous man? He was naturally passionate, both physically and mentally, she knew that both personally and from watching him work—but had that passion always led to a possessive instinct, a jealousy that resisted logic or persuasion?

Mark was absently massaging her cold hands. 'So I suppose he didn't know about the accident for quite a time?'

'He still doesn't,' she said, and Mark did a double-take.

'Didn't you keep in touch with him?'

'I would have written every day, if it hadn't been for the accident, but once I was told I couldn't have children, I only wrote one letter—ending our engagement.'

'What?' Mark's eyes widened. 'But . . . why?'

'Dev wanted to get married because he wanted children, and I couldn't give him any—what else could I do? I had to set him free to find someone else, someone who would give him children.'

'And he accepted that?' Mark's mouth twisted in contempt. 'I wish I'd known all this last time I saw him, I'd have kicked his teeth down his throat! If he had really loved you, he wouldn't have let you go. The man's a bastard.' Then his brows met and he stared at her, scowling. 'But if the engagement is off, why have you been seeing him since he got back to England? And why did he act as if he owned you the other night? The way he was knocking hell out of me, I could have sworn he was jealous of me and hated my guts.'

Megan sighed. 'Mark, I didn't tell him the truth.'

Mark looked bewildered. 'Then what did you tell him? You must have given him some reason for breaking off the engagement?'

'I told him there was another man,' she said, and Mark stared at her in silence for several minutes, shaking his head.

'Why on earth did you do that? What a stupid lie. The man isn't a child, doesn't he deserve the truth?'

She smiled sadly. 'I knew how much he wanted children. I think that was why he proposed. I couldn't let him go ahead and marry me when I knew it would mean the end of any chance of Dev having his own children.'

'So you lied to him?'

'I had to!'

'Couldn't you have given him the benefit of the doubt? Don't you think you owed it to him to let him do his own deciding?'

'It wouldn't have been fair to him to force him to choose between me and the family he wants so badly. I overheard him talking about it to his sister, you see; I know how he feels about me, about having children.'

'Well. *I* wouldn't thank you for refusing to let *me* make my own choice,' Mark said flatly, then his eyes narrowed, a startled look coming into them. 'Hang on! Did he think I was the guy who had taken you away from him? Was that why he knocked me all over the place that night?'

Megan bit her lip. 'I'm afraid so.'

Mark let out a long whistle. 'Well, I don't feel too comfortable about that, Megan. It looks to me as if you've been using me, and I'm not very happy about it.' He stared hard at her, frowning. 'I'm beginning to think I really didn't know you at all. You can be pretty devious, Megan. I'm sorry if that sounds harsh, but I don't approve of the way you've treated Hurst, or, come to that, the way you've manipulated me. I've been set up to hoodwink Hurst, haven't I? I think I ought to go along and see the guy and tell him the truth.'

CHAPTER TEN

'NO, MARK! You can't!' Agitated, Megan grabbed his arm, her fingers biting into it as she stared pleadingly at him. 'Promise me you won't!'

He took some persuading, but reluctantly in the end he did promise to keep her secret. He tried to talk her into coming out for a late supper somewhere, but Megan shook her head.

'I'm very tired, Mark. Can I take a rain-check?'

He surveyed her pale, smudged face and grimaced. 'You look like death.'

She managed a smile. 'Thanks, that makes me feel a lot better!' and Mark looked guilty at once.

'Meggy! I . . .'

'I was teasing,' she said quickly wishing he would go, because she really was barely managing to stay on her feet, and as soon as he had gone she was going to collapse. Perhaps he read it in her face, because he began to walk to the front door almost immediately after that, and Megan went with him, hiding her eagerness to see him go.

He gave her a quick kiss. 'Goodnight, take care of yourself.'

'And you,' she said. 'I'm sorry for . . . everything, Mark.'

'Forget it, I don't blame you,' he said, with an odd look on his face. Mark had been chasing her for weeks, busily trying to turn their friendship into something more, but now all that was over. Mark might have asked her out to supper, but he was only being polite. She wondered wryly how he would have reacted if she had accepted.

She wouldn't be seeing him again, she suspected. Mark was backing out. He knew now that she was in love with Dev, and there was really no point to their relationship, but there was more to it than that. He had just discovered that Megan could not have children; she had seen what a shock that had been to him. Mark had never seemed eager to have children—but he was an artist, and obsessed by perfection. She couldn't have a child, which meant that she was not perfect; she was flawed.

Mark was too nice, and too kind, to want her to realise how he felt, but Megan was ultra-sensitive about what had happened to her. Her intuition picked up all the things he was trying to hide. She wasn't surprised; she didn't even blame him. Mark was reacting the way she was sure Dev would react—with compassion, with concern, but still in shocked dismay. Mark didn't need to feel guilty, that was the difference. He knew that she was not in love with him. He could walk away without shame.

Dev was not in that position. If she told him about the accident and all it meant, and then admitted that she still loved him, Dev would be torn apart by the choice he had to make, and Megan couldn't do that to him. Her love meant she had to shield him, even if it meant bitter

unhappiness for herself. Mark might say that she
should give Dev the chance to choose for
himself, but her woman's instinct told her to
protect her man at all costs. If love was selfish
enough to let a man sacrifice his most cherished
dream, how could it call itself love? she thought,
getting into bed after Mark had gone.

She couldn't get to sleep, though; tossing and
turning, she could only think about Dev, and
that he was going away again in the morning.
She wished she knew whether or not his sister
had found him, and managed to talk him out of
it. Emma Stansfield was a very determined
woman, but Dev was not a man you could push
around or even persuade to change his mind
once his mind was made up.

Megan had never liked Emma. The other girl
was too arrogant and too spoilt, for one thing,
and for another it was hard to like someone who
went out of her way to make it clear that she did
not like you. Megan often wondered why Emma
had taken such an immediate dislike to her. Of
course, when she overheard Dev talking to his
sister she had found out! Emma simply despised
her. She didn't think that a 'plain little nobody'
was good enough to marry into the Hurst family.
Megan had resented it and disliked Emma even
more, but tonight she felt somehow less hostile.

When they'd talked tonight, though, there
had been a flash of understanding between them
for the first time.

It had come when Emma had threatened to kill
her if Dev died out in South America, and

Megan had wearily said that, if Dev died, Emma would be welcome to kill her.

Megan had been beyond trying to hide the unhappiness she felt. Emma had seen it; her face had changed, they had looked at each other for that instant; two women recognising their mutual predicament, the age-old trap of human love.

Megan wished it had come earlier, that possibility of a friendship between herself and Dev's sister. But there was no point in daydreams. Outside fairy-tales, wishes didn't come true.

Leaning over, she picked up the clock from her bedside-table and stared grimly at it. She had been in bed an hour, and was still as far from sleep as ever. Lying down again, she shut her eyes and ordered herself to relax, to stop thinking. It was thinking that was keeping her awake.

When she opened her eyes again it was to see grey light filtering through the curtains. Rolling over, she looked at the time in surprise. Seven o'clock! She must have slept, but it didn't seem to have done her much good. She felt just as terrible as she had last night, especially now that she was conscious and remembered.

Dev was flying back to South America today! She shut her eyes with a stifled groan, then quickly slid out of bed and ran to the bathroom, her stomach heaving. She was going to throw up.

A few minutes later she sat on the rim of the bath, shuddering and still feeling sick, wishing she was dead. In the mirror her face showed green, her tangled hair all over the place.

'What a sight you are!' she told her reflection glumly, and at that moment the front door bell rang in a peremptory fashion.

Her heart turned over. 'Who now?' she asked her face in the mirror. Was it Emma back again, with news of Dev? Or still looking for Dev?

Megan ran back into her bedroom and grabbed up her lacy white négligé, putting it on as she hurried through her flat to the front door.

The bell rang again, louder, just as she pulled the door open. 'Oh, you're not dressed!' Emma Stansfield said with urgency in her tone. 'Look, I just got a call from Dev at last. He's at Heathrow and his plane leaves in an hour. If we hurry we can get there, but you'll have to throw on the first thing you find. There's no time to waste.'

Megan remembered the last time she had rushed to Heathrow to see Dev. Miserably, she began, 'There's no point! He won't listen, and anyway . . .'

'Get dressed, will you?' Emma pushed her forcibly down the corridor, protesting at every step. 'Just run a comb through your hair, forget make-up.' Emma was at her wardrobe, pulling down a turquoise sweater and some jeans. 'Here, these will do. Hurry up.'

'You don't understand,' Megan muttered, opening a drawer to look for underwear. 'Even if we get there, Dev will be in the departure lounge and they won't let us through. This isn't an emergency.'

'Don't keep arguing. If he goes back this early, he'll undo all the work the doctors put in on him.

That isn't guesswork. I have it from the horse's mouth. His specialist rang us to say he was very worried, and to ask us to stop Dev if we could.'

Megan stood still, staring at Emma, her face bloodless. Emma stared back, nodding insistent confirmation. She was pale, too; her eyes were rimmed with pink as if she had been crying, and she had dressed in such a hurry that the buttons on her red striped shirt were half undone. Megan had never seen her look so human and vulnerable, but there was no hesitation in the angry way Emma said to her, 'For God's sake, get on with it!'

Without another word, Megan dressed with shaky hands, washed her face, cleaned her teeth, combed her hair, before Emma rushed her at whirlwind speed out of the flat, into the car parked outside on a yellow line, oblivious of any law-breaking.

'Hold on to your hat,' Emma said, putting her foot down as they drove off.

The car was a sleek sports model with a purring engine. As Megan soon realised, it was capable of incredible speeds.

Her hands gripped the edge of her seat as Emma hurtled along the half-empty roads, but she didn't give vent to the scream of terror locked in her throat. She had doubted if they could get to the airport before the plane left, but then she had had no idea that Dev's sister was a fiendishly daring driver.

Glancing sideways, Emma asked, 'Scared?'

'Petrified,' Megan said. 'But carry on. I don't

mind being killed in a good cause.'

The other woman laughed; her grey eyes bright. 'I love speed, myself. I rarely get a chance to let my baby out for a really good run.'

Megan watched the appalled faces of other drivers as they passed like a flash of light. 'How long do you think it will take us?'

'Fifteen minutes now.' Emma's hair blew in the wind as she gave Megan another quick look. 'I had a call from Mark Bond last night, by the way.'

Stiffening, Megan tried to look indifferent. 'Oh?'

'He told me a surprising story.'

'Mark is a surprising man.' Megan was furious with him.

'Is it true, though?' demanded Emma.

'I don't know what he told you!' Megan was carefully offhand.

'Oh, I think you do!' Emma looked at her again and Megan gave a cry of panic.

'Please! Keep on your eyes on the road if you must go so fast!'

'Don't worry, I know what I'm doing. I used to be a professional driver once.'

Megan gave her an incredulous look. 'Really?' It sounded like fantasy; she had supposed that Emma had married straight from finishing school. She knew Emma had been married for around ten years, and she only looked about thirty, so she must have been very young at the time.

'For a few months!' insisted Emma. 'Until

Graham, my husband, put his foot down. I was good, though, and that isn't just conceit.' She roared round a corner, terrifying a lorry driver, who yelled soundlessly after them. Ignoring him, Emma said crisply, 'So it is true, is it?'

Megan sighed. 'Mark had no business telling you . . . he promised!'

'He said he promised not to tell Dev, but he didn't promise not to tell me!'

'Oh, how could he?'

'He stuck to the letter of the law, that's all,' said Emma. 'What tough luck for you, though. I had no idea you had been involved in an accident.'

Megan was staring at the motorway ahead of them. 'It happened just up the road from here, actually. I was on my way back from the airport the day Dev left and I went into a lorry. Oh, my fault, not the lorry-driver's. I was thinking of other things.'

'Dev?'

'Dev.'

They were almost at the airport and Megan looked at her watch, her stomach full of butterfiles. Were they too late, anyway, though? Dev must surely be in the departure lounge and the security people weren't going to let them through to talk to him.

'I'm sorry,' Emma Stansfield said abruptly, and Megan gave her a blank, uncomprehending look.

'For not being very friendly in the past,' Emma added in a rough, embarrassed voice. 'I'm very fond of my brother and I was afraid he was making another ghastly mistake. I didn't care for Gianna much, even before she bolted with her oilman, but she was quite a beauty, and . . . well . . .'

She was pink and Megan laughed shortly. 'And I'm not! No need to beat around the bush, I know I'm just an ordinary girl.'

'Oh, I don't know,' Emma said. 'You do rather grow on people. You have nice eyes and a lovely smile.'

'Thank you.' Megan was touched and surprised.

'And if you love my brother, I could easily start to think you're beautiful!'

Megan's lips quivered and her eyes filled with tears. 'Oh, I love him, but . . .'

'No buts,' Emma said with a touch of her customary arrogance, then turned into the terminal area.

'I'll drop you, then I'll go and park,' she said as she slotted into the traffic queue. 'With any luck Dev won't have gone through into the departure lounge yet. He said on the phone that there might be a short delay because it was misty earlier. It has obviously cleared now, but Dev said there was a backlog of delayed flights to go before his plane could leave.'

'Emma, listen . . . even if I see him, there's nothing to say—don't you understand? I can't have children, and Dev badly wants to start a family. I can't marry him. And if I don't mean to marry him, what am I doing here? I have no right to ask him not to go.'

'Stop talking nonsense,' Emma bluntly said, pulling up outside the main entrance of the terminal. 'You're here to stop Dev chucking his life away! If he goes back to South America and dies out there, all your noble qualms about not being able to give him children will sound pretty hollow to me, and I think they will to you, then! I realise it must have been a terrible blow to you to find out you couldn't have a baby, and you must still be in utter turmoil and not making much real sense inside your head. But Dev's going back because he thinks you don't love him, and you do, so go and tell him, and stop being such a bloody fool.'

Megan stared at her, open-mouthed, and Emma laughed.

'Get going!' she ordered, and Megan found herself obeying. As she stumbled out of the car Emma shot away, and Megan, still arguing with herself, began to run.

She had never thought that she would ever find herself liking Dev's sister, but then she had never really known Emma until now. There had been a wall between them, but their shared love and fear for Dev had broken it down, and Emma had just been making an astonishing amount of sense. Megan had failed to see the obvious—if Dev went back to South America before he was completely cured, and died out there, she would blame herself for the rest of her life.

The terminal was crowded and blaring with messages on the tannoy. Megan caught sight of the digital clock high above her, and groaned.

Dev's flight left in half an hour; he must be boarding the plane by now. She halted in front of a monitor screen to check, and saw with a leap of the heart that most of the listed flights seemed to have the words delayed next to them. Her eyes fixed on Dev's destination. That, too, was showing as delayed. She began to hurry towards the departures barrier to see if the passengers for that flight had gone through, yet. The huge lounge seemed to be so full of people that perhaps many passengers hadn't been allowed to go through yet.

She was so intent that she ran past Dev without even seeing him until she was a little distance away, when her mind suddenly flashed her the image of him sitting among a lot of other patient people, his hand-luggage at his feet, his face pale and set.

Turning, Megan stared without speaking or moving. Dev hadn't seen her yet. He was in a world of his own; his eyes staring straight ahead, his jaw taut. For all those crowds, he looked so alone; her heart moved painfully inside her and she went back to him, feeling as if she was on the end of a string he was slowly reeling in.

He was casually dressed in a combat-style jacket and dark green cotton trousers, a black cotton shirt and lightweight boots. For the first time she could really imagine him on the Amazon; she remembered the lyrical excitement he had breathed when he talked about it and how much he obviously loved it. Yet from his

face now he could have been going to his
execution. He certainly wasn't overjoyed to be
getting back there.

She halted in front of him, and the others on
the seat stared at her, but at first Dev didn't
seem aware of her, then his eyes focused and
darkened, his pale skin grew paler, his mouth
harder.

'What are you doing here?'

'I came to find you.'

He shrugged, unmoved. 'Emma, I suppose? I
shouldn't have rung to let her know I was
leaving. It didn't occur to me that she would tell
you, of all people. I suppose she bullied you into
coming along to talk me out of going? Well, I'm
afraid you've wasted your time.'

Their audience had listened with interest to
Dev, they then all looked at Megan for her
answer. Aware of this, she grew very flushed,
stammering.

'Can we go and talk outside, in private?'

'No, I want to make sure I don't miss my flight
being called,' said Dev flatly.

'We can't talk here!'

'We don't have anything to talk about!'

'Dev!' she pleaded. 'Please!'

'If you've got something to say to me, say it
here and now, or forget it,' he said in an icy
voice.

He was making it as hard as possible, but even
if she had to talk to him with all these witnesses,
she wasn't backing off this time. She took a long,
deep breath. 'Last time you went off to South

America, I tried to see you . . . talk to you . . . do you remember?'

'I remember,' he said without interest.

'You saw me but you walked away, ignoring me.'

The eyes of their audience widened; they all looked at Dev with reproach, but he still seemed unaware of them, or else it was giving him some sort of kick to force Megan to make these very personal revelations in front of a lot of strangers.

Dev didn't bother to answer at all, and after a pause, Megan said, 'So I drove home, but I didn't get there. I crashed my car.'

Dev did look at her, then; startled, frowning. 'Were you badly hurt?'

The rest of her audience seemed as interested; they were staring at her from head to toe, inspecting her for signs of damage.

'Yes,' she said. 'I was in hospital for months. I hadn't been out long when you came back, in fact.'

'You're OK now, though?' There was a shadow of anxiety in his eyes.

'That's what I want to talk to you about! But I can't talk here. I have to tell you something in private, Dev!'

His brows together, he hesitated, and she gave him a pleading look. 'Please, Dev!' He glanced from side to side, saw the interested faces of their audience, and glowered at them before getting to his feet.

He picked up his hand-luggage and slung it by wide straps from his shoulder, then followed

Megan began towards the entrance. They met Emma coming through the electronic doors and she grinned broadly, unperturbed by the glare she got from her brother.

'Thank heaven for that! You found him.'

'I'll talk to you later!' Dev said menacingly. 'If I have time before I get my plane!'

'Don't be a bigger fool than God made you, Devlin Hurst,' his sister said. 'My car's in the short-stay car park when you want me. I'll drive you both back whenever you're ready.'

'I am going to South America!' he insisted, and Emma just laughed and vanished.

Outside, Dev and Megan walked to one end of the pavement to where there was a low wall. Dev gestured. 'Sit down and tell me whatever you have to say, but make it quick, because I am not missing my plane.'

She sat and gripped and edge of the wall with both hands. The sharp rim of the bricks dug into her flesh, but she barely noticed that. 'After the crash I had an operation,' she said without preamble. She made a face at him. 'I have to say this and there's no easy way, so I'll just have to blurt it out or I won't say it at all. I had my womb removed.'

Dev stood there, staring at her. If he had seemed pale before, he looked like old grey parchment now, and Megan put out her hands and took hold of his cold fingers, wanting to cry.

'Don't look like that! I'm sorry, Dev.'

His fingers tightened around hers until she almost cried out with the pain. He swore and she winced. 'You're sorry!' he ground out harshly.

'I knew you would take it like this,' she whispered, watching him sadly. 'That's why I didn't tell you before, I had to lie to you, make an excuse for not marrying you, so that you wouldn't feel you had to . . .'

'Lie to me?' he cried out in a low, hoarse voice. 'You lied . . . this was why you wrote and said you couldn't marry me?' Before she could reply he answered himself in that strange, almost frightening voice, 'Of course—and there wasn't anyone else, no other man?'

She shook her head dumbly.

'What about . . .' be began, and she answered without waiting for him to finish.

'Mark? No, he was just a friend, I lied about that, too, to throw you off the scent.'

He suddenly caught her face between his long, thin fingers and stared down at her fixedly. She wasn't sure how she had expected him to react, but it hadn't been with such bitter anger.

'You lied to me? How could you? I ought to hit you,' he broke out thickly. 'Something this bad happens to you and you don't tell me! Worse, you lie to me? I should have been here, been with you! You went through this hell all on your own? Why did you shut me out? You knew I loved you, for God's sake!'

'I didn't,' she said in a still, flat voice, and Dev's grey eyes flashed.

'How can you say that? I'd asked you to marry me!'

'Yes, that night at the party at your family

home,' she said quietly. 'But I practically had to propose to you first and even then you seemed very reluctant. I could see you weren't very sure, and you didn't tell me you loved me—it was all very half-hearted, and then I overheard you talking to your sister.'

He frowned. 'You shouldn't take any notice of what Emma says—her bark is far worse than her bite. When you get to know her better you'll like her.'

'I think I do already.' Megan gave a faint smile, then sighed. 'But it wasn't what Emma said that really upset me, it was what you said.'

Dev's face was blank. 'What did I say?'

'That you wanted children; you said you needed a family and a home, and I would give you those, even though I was just a plain little nobody.'

'I could never have said that!' He was either acting brilliantly, or he was amazed, but Megan couldn't believe that look of bafflement.

'You did, Dev! Don't lie about it! I heard you say it!'

Dev was looking furious now; his eyes glittering. 'I don't know what you think you heard, I just know I never said anything of the sort. I couldn't have done because I have never thought you were either plain or a little nobody. I'm sick with love for you. Sick with it, Megan.' He said it through clenched teeth, as if it was an insult he was throwing at her, as if he hated her, rather than loved her, and yet her heart sang wildly.

Dev stared into her eyes, breathing as if there was no air, and Megan felt hot colour pouring up her face at the way he watched her.

He looked around, making a desperate noise. 'We can't talk here!'

'Emma said she would wait for us in the . . .'

'Damn Emma, let's take a taxi.'

'But she'll wonder where we are!'

'Let her wonder.' He seized her hand and began to drag her away and Megan went, protesting.

'Emma brought me here, you can't do this, Dev, it isn't fair to her. She'll wait there for hours before she realises we've gone without her.'

'She'll work it out. She isn't stupid, that's half her trouble—too damn clever by half.' He bundled her into a taxi, still talking, and gave the driver his address.

'Oh, your luggage!' Megan suddenly remembered, looking back at the disappearing airport. 'It will be on the plane! Shouldn't you go back and do something to stop it going off to South America?'

'Let it go,' he shrugged, his arm curving around her shoulders. 'It doesn't matter. I'll deal with it later. At the moment, I've got something more important on my mind.' He bent towards her, his eyes fixed on her mouth.

Megan gave the taxi driver a glance and went pink as she caught him watching them in his mirror. 'Dev!' she whispered, and Dev looked that way too, grimacing.

'This is going to be the longest taxi ride of my life!'

'We have to talk, anyway,' she said, her voice very low.

Dev watched her. 'Do we? I thought we'd talked enough, myself.'

'I came this morning because I don't want you to go back to the Amazon until you're really well, Dev, but nothing has changed—I still can't marry you.'

'Why not?'

'You know why not. I told you.'

'You told me you've had to have your womb removed, but I don't see why that means you can't marry me!'

Megan looked desperately at him, her lashes wet with slow tears. 'Of course you do. You're just being kind and sorry for me, but you know you want children, a family . . .'

'We'll adopt.'

'You'll want children of your own, Dev!'

'I want you.' His fingertips caressed her cheek and she shivered, closing her eyes.

'No, Dev.'

'Yes, I do, and when we're alone in my flat I'll show you just how much I want you.'

Her blood ran hotly and she shuddered with desire as she heard that note in his voice. She couldn't bear the thought of losing him; she wanted him with the same hunger and she turned her burning face into his shoulder, whispering, because she dared not say this out loud. They were talking in very low voices, but the taxi driver might still overhear them, and Megan couldn't bear anyone to hear what she was going to say now. 'I'll go to bed with you, I'll live with you until you're tired of me, but I won't marry you, Dev.'

He drew in air audibly, as though she had just punched him in the stomach. 'Darling!' His hand came down on her hair, stroked it lingeringly, his cheek lowered down towards the thick, dark strands he was fondling. 'The most immoral and wonderful thing anyone ever said to me,' he whispered with a smile in his voice.

'I'm serious, Dev, I mean it!' she insisted, trembling.

'I'm glad to hear it, but I want you on a more long-term basis,' he said, his fingers twining in her hair and tugging to make her look up at him.

Megan's face was burning as she met his eyes. 'I hope you realise that I'm not in the habit of making that sort of proposition to men,' she muttered.

'I should hope not!' He dropped a light kiss on her nose. 'But I can see I shall have to marry you to save you from this tendency to make impulsive offers in taxis.'

That made her laugh, as he'd intended, but her eyes sobered quickly. 'Oh, Dev, you haven't really thought this out, you haven't realised what it would mean. How can I deprive you of having your own children? You might come to resent me, you might . . .'

'Get run over in the street tomorrow,' he finished for her. 'Life is full of imponderables. We just have to deal with the certainties we know, and one of those is that I love you and don't want to have to spend the rest of my life without you. How about you?'

'Oh, I don't know . . .' she wailed. 'I don't want you to come to hate me one day.'

He watched her ruefully. 'How can I convince you?' He ran a hand over her hair, then exclaimed, 'Wait a minute!' and to her disbelief started to unbutton his shirt.

'Dev, what on earth are you doing?' She shot a look at the taxi driver's back, but he was busy watching the crowded road ahead, thank goodness, and hadn't noticed. Megan caught hold of Dev's hand and hissed, 'Stop it! Not here. Wait until we get to your flat.'

He grinned at her. 'This won't wait.' Holding her hand captive he slid his other hand inside his shirt and pulled out a plain silver locket on a matching chain. Megan stared, bewildered.

Dev clicked the locket open and held it out to her. Inside were a small circular photograph of her, taken by Dev not long before he first went to the Amazon, and curled around it the dark strands of the lock of hair he had cut from her head the night he proposed.

Megan stared at them in utter silence, then Dev clicked the locket shut and put it back inside his shirt.

'I've carried that around for months. You see, I love you very much, Megan. I've been in love before; you know all about Gianna. That was a very bad experience and it made me wary; it made me a potentially jealous and suspicious man, too. I was jealous when I saw you with Mark Bond that night.'

'I told you the truth, Dev . . .' she began anxiously, and he nodded.

'I believe you, but at the time I didn't want to listen to any explanation because it had all welled up inside me. You can't imagine it, Megan—it's a terrible feeling, as black as hell. I rushed away because I was hurting too much to stay there, and when you came to the airport in the morning I still couldn't bear to talk in case you saw it. I was ashamed of how I felt; jealousy is a sickness. But I still loved you; I still wore my locket and I would have written if you had written to me, but no letter came, and when it did I was too ill to do anything about it, and I knew I'd be coming home, soon, anyway.'

She looked quickly at him, and he made a wry face. 'You don't think for one moment that I ever intended to leave it like that? I was still feeling very low when I first got back, but I was going to come and find you as soon as I felt strong enough, then I saw you at that party and I knew right away that nothing had changed, I still felt the same way, and it wasn't long before I'd convinced myself that you did, too. We hadn't known each other well enough before I left, I thought. You had been attracted, but the feeling you had hadn't had a chance to grow roots. If I stayed around and we saw each other often enough, this time we would make it.'

'You should have said all this before, Dev! I've

been working in the dark for too long. You're
much too secretive. How could I guess what you
thought and felt when you went out of your way
to hide it from me?'

'I'll never hide anything from you again,
Megan, if you promise to tell me the honest truth
about how you feel, in future!'

She searched his face with desperate eyes,
wondering what to say. Dev had somehow
manipulated her to this point, in spite of all her
firm intentions about saying goodbye to him.
She felt herself weakening, her grasp on that
common-sense decision slipping. His eyes were
brilliant with feeling as they stared back at her,
and she gave a long sigh.

'I love you, Dev,' she capitulated. It might be
folly, it might be selfish, but she needed him
badly and she would do everything in her power
to make him happy.

Dev leaned forward in urgent silence and they
kissed passionately, their arms around each
other, while the fascinated taxi driver watched in
his mirror, but by then they were in a world of
their own and had forgotten everyone else
existed.

Harlequin Presents.

Coming Next Month

Available in October wherever paperback books are sold, or through Harlequin Reader Service:

In the U.S.
901 Fuhrmann Blvd.
P.O. Box 1397
Buffalo, N.Y. 14240-1397

In Canada
P.O. Box 603
Fort Erie, Ontario
L2A 5X3

Have You Ever Wondered If You Could Write A Harlequin Novel?

Here's great news—Harlequin is offering a series of cassette tapes to help you do just that. Written by Harlequin editors, these tapes give practical advice on how to make your characters—and your story—come alive. There's a tape for each contemporary romance series Harlequin publishes.

Mail order only

All sales final
